He was too close—deliberately close— as if he wanted that closeness so his body could talk to hers.

Or was it nothing more than politeness on his part and the only body doing any talking was hers? Talking to *her*...telling her it was enjoying the closeness.

Surely not!

They reached the vehicle and something in the way he regarded her seemed to suggest it *hadn't* only been her body.

Desperate to get all thoughts of the man and the way her body was reacting to him out of her head, she went for lightness.

'And will we have to ruffle up the big marriage bed every morning to make it look as if we've slept in it?'

The look he was giving her intensified, and a small smile played around his lips.

'I didn't say *I* wouldn't use the bed,' he murmured, and a shiver of pure excitement ran down Kate's spine.

More likely it was fear, her head muttered as she hauled herself up into the passenger seat in an attempt to escape both the man and the feelings he was generating in her body.

And she was tired—emotions were always more raw when one was tired.

But was attraction stronger? Particularly unwanted attraction?

Why would it be?

Of course it had to be the tiredness. Why else would she be feeling it...?

Dear Reader

Books come together in many ways—a little bit here and a little bit there. One of the 'bits' this time has now become legend in my family. Some forty years ago my mother-in-law went to see a woman who read cards to tell the future, and this woman told her that if she went away on a trip with her widowed son and his two teenage daughters she'd never have to worry about him again.

That night the son in question phoned her from interstate, where he lived, to ask her to go to India with him and the girls. She agreed—here was the trip the cards had foretold! I joined their flight in far-off Western Australia as the tour leader, and that's how I met my husband and the two teenagers who have become my very loved daughters.

It still gives me shivers up the spine when I realise just how little we know of the part fate must play in our lives. I do hope fate is kind to *you*.

Meredith Webber

THE SHEIKH DOCTOR'S BRIDE

BY
MEREDITH WEBBER

First published in Great Britain 2015
by Mills & Boon, an imprint of Harlequin (UK) Limited,
Large Print edition 2015
Eton House, 18-24 Paradise Road,
Richmond, Surrey, TW9 1SR

© 2015 Meredith Webber

ISBN: 978-0-263-25494-5

Harlequin (UK) Limited's policy is to use papers that are natural, renewable and recyclable products and made from wood grown in sustainable forests. The logging and manufacturing processes conform to the legal environmental regulations of the country of origin.

Printed and bound in Great Britain
by CPI Antony Rowe, Chippenham, Wiltshire

Meredith Webber says of herself, 'Once I read an article which suggested that Mills & Boon® were looking for new Medical Romance™ authors. I had one of those "I can do that" moments, and gave it a try. What began as a challenge has become an obsession—though I do temper the "butt on seat" career of writing with dirty but healthy outdoor pursuits, fossicking through the Australian Outback in search of gold or opals. Having had some success in all of these endeavours, I now consider I've found the perfect lifestyle.'

Recent titles by Meredith Webber:

PROLOGUE

FAREED IBN JADYM IBN MUSTAFFAH FARUKE eyed the green country through which he travelled with distaste. Not that he didn't appreciate green. The shiny, almost luminous green of date-palm fronds around an oasis was always a welcome sight, and contrasted brilliantly with the red desert sand through which one had to travel to see them.

But green everywhere, everything green, apart from white paint splashed haphazardly on the fence posts lining the drive down which they now travelled.

Why, in the name of all that was holy, was his uncle coming to this run-down establishment, stuck out in a swathe of green, miles from the city in which they'd been staying?

So his uncle wanted to buy a horse—wanted him, Fareed, to see the horse before the purchase—but could not the horse have come to them? Ibrahim wasn't one to go out of his way for anything or any-one, however much he loved his horses.

But Fareed's apprehension about what was going on with his uncle went beyond this trip to a horse stud. Something was brewing in his uncle's devious mind, and Fareed had a disturbing suspicion that the 'something' was to do with him.

Why else would his uncle insist he take leave from the hospital to accompany him on this trip to Australia?

To buy a *horse*!

And why had Thalia, an old crone who lived somewhere in the palace compound and was said to read the future from marks in the sand, or oil poured on a cup of water, been spending so much time with his uncle prior to this trip? Thalia claimed she was a *kahin*, from a line of female fortune-tellers that went back into ancient times.

Surely his uncle, English educated, graduate of Oxford and with a further business degree from Harvard, didn't still believe in the words of a sooth-sayer?

Fareed shook his head, sorry he was in the lead of the four cars and couldn't ask his uncle these questions. Then something flashed past the window and soothsayers and his uncle's devious plans were forgotten.

The horse was a dark caramel in colour, its mane nearly white. It was pounding up the slight slope of a track on the other side of the fence, and on its back, her face alight with the joy of speed, sat a slim woman, taller than most jockeys but riding with her legs tucked up, her body bent along the horse's neck, flame-coloured hair flying out behind her—a woman at one with the animal.

A painting of the image might be called *Freedom*, and though Fareed yearned for freedom, duty was a stronger master. Oh, for a while he was okay, working in the hospital, doing what he enjoyed, feeling needed and appreciated, and although, when he *did* succeed his uncle to the Sultanate, he hoped to continue his medical career at least part-time, he knew his duty was to his people, and to helping them come to terms with the changing world in which they now lived.

But the beauty of the horse and its rider had eased some of Fareed's apprehension about this trip. Perhaps he should, as Ibrahim kept insisting, simply relax and enjoy the last few days of this break away from work. And, really, was green all that bad a colour?

* * *

The man Kate's mother was hoping would save the family's stables arrived in a fleet of long black limousines—if four exceedingly large vehicles could be called a fleet.

According to her mum, he was some kind of Eastern potentate—she read a lot, her mum!

The arrival of the sleek vehicles suggested he might be a very wealthy potentate, though no doubt a con man would have made an equally impressive arrival, Kate told herself.

Cynical?

Kate?

No more so than any other thirty-two-year-old woman who'd grown up with a dearly loved father who had always had a fortune waiting for him just around the next corner; no more so than any other woman who had recently been dumped by a long-term lover who couldn't believe she would go home to be with her mother after said father's death, instead of staying with him on the other side of the world.

She turned Marac and headed back to the stables. Mum would offer the potentate some tea so she, Kate, would have time to give the horse a good rub-down and settle him in his stall before the inspection party arrived.

Cantering back down the hill, watching the cars wending their way down the drive, she wondered about the future. *If* the potentate saved the stables, would she go back to the US, to Mark? Could she go back to a man with so little empathy?

She'd been home two months now, time enough to see the man she'd thought she loved through clearer eyes. No, going back to Mark was not an option.

But, then, if this potentate didn't buy Tippy, she wouldn't have to think about options.

Kate tried to see her home through the visitors' eyes: the lush paddocks shaded by wide spreading gum trees and filled with spectacular horses; the green fields; the placid stream running through the valley; the old stone and bleached-wood stables; and, by the stream, the house, built from stones hauled from the creek over a hundred years ago...

Her mother's—no, in fact, it was Billy's heritage...

CHAPTER ONE

THE IMAGE OF the girl on the horse was still vivid in Fareed's mind as the vehicles rolled to a stop in a big paved area outside the stone-built house. A middle-aged woman had been waiting at the gate and she stepped forward as the entourage began to emerge from the vehicles.

And Fareed wondered again about his uncle's insistence on travelling everywhere with this entourage. Surely Ibrahim and the stud manager, with Fareed tagging along, could manage to buy a horse. But, no, a fleet of vehicles seemed to accompany them everywhere, with dour-faced palace guards, who probably hated green as much as he did, hovering protectively around his uncle at all times.

Preventing an attack from a rabid kangaroo?

The driver was already opening the door for Ibrahim, while the men in their unaccustomed garb of dark suits alighted from the other cars and stood erect, in a kind of deferential arc around where Ibrahim would appear.

Did he do it to impress people?

Fareed doubted that, for Ibrahim was the most modest of men, and rarely made a show of his position. No, there was definitely some hidden agenda in this trip to Australia, and he, Fareed, was completely in the dark about it. He stood beside his uncle as the woman approached, wishing he could read what was going on behind the bland but still charming smile.

'I'm Sally Walker. Welcome to Dancing Waters Stud. The river runs over rounded granite stones on the bend below the house and the waters seem to dance, which is where it got its name.'

She sounded nervous and her arm shook slightly as she offered her hand to Ibrahim. To Fareed's surprise, his uncle not only took it but raised it to his lips for a swift courtly kiss.

Sally Walker blushed a fiery red and Fareed felt a momentary pang of pity for her.

'Sultan Ibrahim ibn—' His uncle broke off the recitation of his name and smiled at her. 'You do not need to know the rest. We call ourselves son of our father—that is the "ibn"—then "ibn" again because he was the son of his father, and I could go on until next week just saying my name. You must call me Ibrahim.'

Hmm! Ibrahim at his most charming!

Fareed's suspicions grew.

'You would like tea or coffee, or a cool drink?' their hostess offered.

'Perhaps later, my dear,' Ibrahim said. 'But first the horses.'

The woman led the way to the stables, explaining as she went.

'The property was developed by my great-grandparents, and while their main interest was in breeding, my grandfather decided to try his hand at training and did very well. Not many horses, because the breeding side of the business was still important, but he found a special thrill in training his own horses, and that must have passed down in the blood to my father and myself.'

They reached the door of the long, low building, redolent of horse and hay and tack and polish. Some trick of the sun's position sent a beam of light into the dark shadows at the end, catching a slim, lithe woman bending and straightening as she brushed down the palomino Fareed had seen earlier. Caught in the ray of light, the pair took on a shining luminosity—something from a painting by an old master, Titian perhaps, given the colour of her hair coming alive in the light.

Fareed paused, riveted by the sight, while beside him Ibrahim seemed to suck in his breath. The girl straightened up and Fareed noticed Ibrahim nod to himself, as if satisfied about something—very satisfied...

The mystery of this trip to Australia deepened.

Damn, they were here before she'd finished. Never mind, she'd give Marac another rub this afternoon.

Kate straightened up, aware she'd have wisps of straw in her hair and smudges on her face and would smell of horse, but knowing she needed to be by her mother's side through this fraught process.

She led Marac into a stall, checked he had food and water, half shut his door, then rubbed her handkerchief over her face and hands and went to meet the visitors.

There was a phalanx of dark, swarthy men around a slightly shorter man. All wore immaculately tailored suits and stern expressions. Except for one, taller than the others—tall, dark and handsome personified, in fact—whose expression was more one of disdain. And his suit was better cut, though he didn't owe those broad shoulders to his tailor. She checked his face again and saw a classic profile—long, straight nose, broad forehead and a firm chin.

You missed the lips, a voice inside her head whispered, but she hadn't missed the lips, not in any way. In fact, it had been the lips that had drawn her attention...

He was still looking disdainful, she reminded herself.

Perhaps he felt visiting a small horse breeder's property was beneath him?

'This is my daughter, Kate,' Sally said. 'Kate, this is Sultan Ibrahim and a lot of other names he says we needn't bother with.'

Kate approached the group and held out her hand to the sultan—didn't sultans wear golden turbans?—then remembered where she'd been and withdrew her hand.

'Sorry, I smell of horse. I really thought I'd be done earlier and cleaned up before you came, but Marac needed the extra run and it was such a beautiful morning, I couldn't resist.'

She smiled hopefully at the sultan, who not only

returned her smile but didn't back away from her eau de horse.

'Well, don't let me keep you from your tour of inspection. I'll tag along behind in case Mum needs anything.'

She slid past the men, telling herself not to look at faces, but how could she not just sneak a peek now she was closer to Mr Handsome—fine-cut features, a long aquiline nose, cheekbones as sharp as razors, lips—best she didn't check out the lips...

She couldn't help glancing up as she passed him, drawn by something more than his expression. Drawn by something she didn't really understand, though it felt vaguely like attraction. Think about the disdain, she told herself, although perhaps it was disgust, not disdain, probably because of the pervading odour of horse that hung around her?

Could she dash up to the house and shower? So she wouldn't smell like horse if she was close to the man again? Was she mad? Attracted to a man like that? And, anyway, she couldn't leave the party now.

Not really, not if Mum might need her.

Or Billy.

Where *was* Billy?

The ache that rarely went away, tucked into a corner of her heart—the ache that was Billy, gentle, sensitive, slow-to-develop Billy—reminded her of the problems that lay ahead.

Face troubles when they come, girl, she remembered her father telling her, and although he always took the words a little too literally, she felt somehow comforted.

Ibrahim had paused by a half-open door and was talking quietly to the inquisitive gelding who'd poked his head out of his stall. As far as Kate could tell, the visitor wasn't speaking English but the horse seemed to understand him anyway and was nodding and holding his head sideways for a hard rub.

'Shamus is Tippy's—Dancing Tiptoes's—older brother—full brother, doing well in local two-year-olds' races.'

The young horse shifted his attention to Kate's mother and nuzzled her neck as she explained.

'You've tried him in the city?' asked one of the entourage—the taller one who'd failed to hide his disdain.

Sally Andrews shook her head.

'Since...'

She faltered and Kate, who knew exactly how huge a strain this meeting was on her mother, stepped in.

'Since my father died two months ago, my mother hasn't wanted to travel far,' she said, speaking directly to the man who'd asked the question, meeting the challenge in his eyes that seemed to peer right into her soul. 'And logistically it's difficult. One of our stable hands was killed in the same accident, so we're short-handed even with me here.'

The questioner's eyes, dark as obsidian, studied her intently.

Suspiciously?

She shook off the tremor of unease his look had caused and concentrated on the main man—Ibrahim.

'So, should I purchase Dancing Tiptoes and wish him to run in the best races, I will have to find another trainer?' Ibrahim asked.

He was standing so close to Sally he must have seen her reaction, and noticed Kate reach out to steady her mother.

Obsidian Eyes certainly had; he missed nothing.

Which might explain, Kate decided, why he, of all the entourage, made her feel so uncomfortable.

'Come and meet him,' she said, determined to ignore the stranger. 'There's no point in discussing training arrangements if you don't like the look of him.'

But who wouldn't? she thought, and her gut clenched as the ramifications of losing Tippy spun in her head.

It was inevitable that Billy would be down in the paddock with Tippy, running alongside him as if they were a pair of the same species.

'My son, Billy,' Sally said, and Ibrahim nodded.

Kate, whose eyes had gone to Ibrahim's face as soon as she saw Billy in the paddock, realised that the man had seen and understood a difference in Billy—seen, understood and accepted! An empathetic man!

Bother the man who was making her uncomfortable, Ibrahim was the boss. It was he who'd decide.

Sally's whistle had brought Tippy to the fence, Billy following more slowly, his natural caution with strangers holding him back.

Or did he understand more about Tippy's future than Kate and Sally realised?

Sally had thrust her hand into the capacious pockets of her trousers, but Ibrahim was faster, producing from the pocket in his immaculate pinstriped suit a small, rosy apple.

'I may?' he said to Sally, who nodded and tucked the sugar lumps back into her pocket.

Tippy studied the stranger almost as warily as Billy had, then threw his head back and snorted before lowering it to lip the apple delicately off the man's hand.

'He likes apples best of all.' Billy had come gradually closer and now stood beside the horse, his too-thin face radiating the love he felt for the animal.

'I do, too,' Ibrahim said. 'Where I live it is hard to grow apples, so when I come to your country I eat as many as possible.'

'Where is it that you can't grow apples?'

'A place called Amberach, far across the sea. A very small place compared to Australia.'

'Did you come here in a plane?'

Kate was aware of her mother's tension returning. Once involved in a conversation, Billy could talk for hours. Should they cut him off?

She glanced at Ibrahim, who showed no sign of impatience—no sign of anything except, she rather thought, simple kindness.

'Yes, I came on a plane.'

'Next to horses I like planes best. Dad always said one day I could go on a plane with the horses, but Dad died, you know.'

'Yes, I did know that,' Ibrahim said gently, while Kate held her breath.

Please, don't offer him a plane ride, especially if you don't mean it.

But Ibrahim's attention was back on the horse—or was he diverting Billy?

'Would you run him again for me?' Ibrahim asked, and Billy whistled to Tippy and the pair took off, Billy understanding what was needed and circling in the middle while Tippy raced around the paddock, his delight in movement lending wings to his feet.

'A truly beautiful sight,' Ibrahim murmured. He turned to one of his men—not the tall, disdainful one. 'He is everything you said he was.'

The man nodded.

'Would you like a cool drink or a cup of tea or coffee?' Kate offered, trying to hide the excitement she was feeling, although she knew her mother would be more apprehensive than excited.

Selling Tippy was one thing—the money from

the sale would save the stables—but keeping him to train—her mother's long-held dream—was quite another.

'First we might walk around a little, see the other horses, the training track and the hill run I've heard about. Dancing Tiptoes was bred here—the mare is here?' Ibrahim replied.

'In foal again, and with the other mares,' Sally told him. 'When they're pregnant they seem to like the company. We'll walk this way.'

She led the party, Ibrahim close behind her, Kate and the entourage bringing up the rear.

'You'd already seen the horse?' she said to the man beside her—the one to whom Ibrahim had turned earlier.

'I was at your father's funeral, then came back here with others,' he said quietly. 'I know it is late to be offering condolences but I am sorry for your loss.'

Kate thanked him and lagged behind, caught off guard by his sudden kindness. She remembered little of that terrible day beyond a blur of cars and people and a need to be strong for both her mother and Billy, yet being uselessly emotional all day.

In fact, it had been Billy who'd been strong for her, and for their mother.

Maybe he would understand more than they thought if Tippy was sold and moved to another trainer. Maybe he'd transfer his love to a new foal—

'Ka-a-a-a-te!'

Her mother's anguished cry brought her out of her reverie. Looking up, she realised the entourage was now some way ahead of her. But instinct had her running down towards the brood mares' paddock, pushing through the phalanx of minders, seeing the taller man, eyes nearly swollen shut, red welts appearing on his face, pulling at his tie, his collar, trying to say something that sounded like 'knife'.

'He wants a knife,' one of the men said, while Kate grabbed the man, trying to ease him to the ground, issuing orders as she did it.

'Call an ambulance—emergency number is triple zero here—and you…' she pointed to the closest '…run up to the stables and get the first-aid box. One of the stable hands will find it for you.'

The stricken man was still struggling to talk, pointing at his throat and making gargling noises.

'What's his name?' she asked Ibrahim, who was looking so pale Kate feared she'd have two patients.

'Fareed,' Ibrahim whispered.

'Don't worry, he'll be all right,' Kate assured the older man, before turning back to her patient.

'Okay, Fareed, I need you to relax. Lie right back, you'll be all right.'

She'd fallen to her knees beside him as she spoke, straightening him out on the ground as best she could when he was still struggling, pushing at her and trying to talk.

'Lie still, you big lunk,' she yelled, and apparently shocked him into immobility. Seizing her chance, she tilted back his head in case CPR became necessary, automatically feeling for a pulse, counting his breaths, more gasps than breaths.

'He was waving his hands then started gasping,' Sally was explaining, but Kate had already found the tiny sting the bee had left behind, barely visible on the lobe of the man's right ear.

'It's anaphylactic shock,' she said as she pulled the sting out and felt in the man's pockets for a pen. 'Did any of you know he had allergies? That he was allergic to bee stings?'

The men looked blankly at her but there was no time to explain.

Tilting the patient's head farther back, she leaned

forward, refusing to even consider the lips she was about to touch as anything other than an anonymous patient's. Although as she closed her mouth over his, breathing air into his lungs, trying to force it in through a passage she knew would be closing more and more, a shiver of something she couldn't understand ran down her spine.

Between breaths she reassured her patient, who was nearly comatose but still struggling, though feebly, against her.

It was Billy who brought the first-aid kit, and Kate, knowing an ambulance would take at least another twenty minutes to reach the property, didn't hesitate.

Opening the big case, she searched for the epinephrine injection she'd told her father to keep there. Either he hadn't bothered or it had been used, emptied and not replaced. She found a scalpel, still in its sterile wrapping, and a small roll of plastic tubing—heaven only knew its real use. Using scissors, she cut a small piece then pulled on gloves.

The skin on the man's neck was smooth and tanned, and her hand hesitated for a fraction of a second but she knew what had to be done.

She'd drawn the scalpel from its sheath and

moved her hand towards that smooth, tanned skin, when one of the entourage stepped forward and, to her astonishment, pulled out a gun.

A small gun, but no less deadly than a big one would be, of that she was sure.

He muttered something at her in his own language and Kate turned to Ibrahim.

'His throat has swollen and he can't breathe— I need to make a hole and breathe into it for him until he can manage on his own. I am a doctor, I can do this.'

Ibrahim nodded and apparently translated but the gun didn't disappear back to wherever it had come from.

So if I do this wrong, he shoots me? Kate wondered in the distant part of her brain not focused on the job.

Feeling carefully, she found the space between his thyroid cartilage and the cricoid cartilage. The scalpel blade bit cleanly, a cut barely half an inch deep, and she slipped her finger into it to open it, before sliding the tube into place.

Ignoring the muttering going on around her and the distant yowling of an ambulance, she bent low and breathed into the tube. Two quick breaths, pause, another breath, pause…

The man's chest was rising so she'd got the tube in successfully, but he needed treatment—epinephrine to combat the shock, hospitalisation for at least twenty-four hours, and minor surgery to repair the gash she'd made in his throat.

Somehow she didn't think she'd have to worry about Billy missing Tippy. These people would want nothing more to do with the Andrews family.

The ambos, once they'd given the patient an epinephrine injection in his thigh, were audibly impressed by her efforts.

'Learnt about it, of course,' one said, 'but never had to do it.'

'I'm an ER doctor,' Kate explained, as they expertly attached monitors to their patient, then lifted him onto the stretcher. 'Though *I've* only had to do it once before so I was a bit shaky.'

'ER doc?' the second man said, when he'd strapped Fareed onto the stretcher. 'Don't suppose you'd come with us—sit with him just in case.'

'I think that would be an excellent idea,' Ibrahim said, and to emphasise the point he actually nodded towards the man who'd held the gun.

Or maybe that was her imagination running riot after the little bit of drama!

Whatever! Someone would have to sit with him to hold the plastic tube in place and it might as well be her. She climbed into the back of the ambulance beside Fareed, who was breathing, somewhat raspily, through the hole in his neck. His eyes opened, the drug taking almost immediate effect, and his hand lifted to feel his neck.

Kate caught the hand before he could dislodge the tube, and held it in hers so it could do no harm. It was a strong hand, with long, lean fingers that fought against her hold—a manly hand...

She put the distraction down to her own shock—*and* disappointment.

'You've suffered anaphylactic shock. You've got a tube in your throat so you can breathe and you've had an injection of epinephrine, which will combat the shock. Now you know you're allergic to bee stings, you should carry a pen with the drug in it wherever you go.'

The disdain she'd read in his eyes earlier returned, so blatant she wanted to turn away.

And let him get away with it?

'Not that I expect gratitude or anything for saving your life, but a smile wouldn't hurt!'

Fortunately, before she could let off any more steam, which she knew was nothing more than a release of her own tension, they drew up at the hospital.

A woman was beside him—a woman in big glasses and flaming red hair she hid in a plait, but nice skin—creamy skin, skin you'd like to touch but preferably when she wasn't going on and on at him. Fareed closed his eyes and tried to clear his head.

She was holding his hand.

He must know her.

She looked angry, but, then, he knew any number of angry women, though none he could remember with plaited hair. Her glasses magnified pale green eyes. Beautiful eyes, he rather thought—even angry, they were special. But the glasses were appalling, although the frames were the same colour as the little freckles sprinkled over her nose.

He was reasonably sure he didn't know any woman with freckles on her nose—well, not freckles that she left on show for everyone to see.

Men's voices and a door opening somewhere near

his feet brought memory of what had happened rushing back. He tried again to feel his throat but the woman stopped him.

'You're at the hospital now. You'll be okay, you'll be fine. They'll want to keep you overnight, to check you haven't had a reaction to the drug, and they'll stitch up the hole I made in your neck, and—'

He freed his hand and put it up to touch her lips, to quiet her, then he smiled to show her he'd understood.

She looked so surprised—by his smile?—his next smile became a genuine one.

After all, she *had* saved his life!

Kate alighted from the ambulance, shaken by what was nothing more than a stranger's casual finger touching her lips. Before she could analyse the reaction, she realised that Ibrahim and his entourage were already there. The older man was watching anxiously as the ambulance men rolled the stretcher out, set it on its legs and began to wheel it away.

He walked beside it, talking to Fareed, obviously concerned about his health, asking questions of the nurse who appeared, giving orders to his men—a caring man.

A sultan?

The word was redolent of fairy stories from Kate's youth—men with golden turbans and casks of glowing jewellery. Did the world still have sultans?

Although it wasn't stature but money that had everyone running around after him, she decided less than an hour later when a specialist ear, nose and throat surgeon arrived from Sydney, helicoptered in to the helipad behind the hospital.

'I'm under orders to stay until the tube comes out and I'm sure he's breathing safely without it—which is now—and then to fix the hole you made,' the man said to Kate after he'd seen the patient. 'My mother could have fixed the hole with one of her embroidery needles. Who *is* this bloke?'

Kate shrugged.

'He came with Sultan Ibrahim to see one of my mother's horses, that's all I know. They must have got on to someone at their consulate and arranged to have you flown here.'

She hesitated, not sure whether to tell the surgeon about the gun. Decided not to. He'd see it for himself if he displeased the entourage in any way.

'Well, now you're here I'll leave him in your expert hands and go home,' she said, then smiled. 'A top ENT man sitting in a country hospital watching a patient recover from anaphylactic shock—that must be a change for you!'

He smiled back.

'Actually, it's all in a good cause. They bribed me with the offer of a very handsome donation to my favourite research programme.'

'Fair enough,' Kate said, aware the man had expected her to ask what it was and to stay for a chat, but she was suddenly overwhelmingly tired and had yet to work out how she was going to get home.

One of the sultan's men sorted that problem, emerging from one of the limos as she came down the hospital steps and opening the rear door for her to get in.

He's either going to kidnap me or take me home, and right now I'm too tired to care, she thought as she climbed into the luxury vehicle and sank back into the soft leather seat.

'Thank you,' she said, as the limo pulled away from the hospital, then the build-up of stress she'd been feeling all day—apprehension about the important man's visit, worry over Billy should Tippy be sold, the medical drama and the strangely attractive disdainful man—seeped silently out of her body, and she rested her head back and closed her eyes.

CHAPTER TWO

KATE AND BILLY were clearing fallen branches from the top paddocks when the fleet of cars rolled back down the drive the next morning—three limos this time, not four.

Wet and filthy, Kate pushed her straggling hair back off her face and scowled as they passed.

'Mum's down in the bottom paddock,' Billy said, and Kate's scowl deepened.

Filthy or not, she'd have to greet the visitors.

Leaving Billy to finish the work, she climbed the fence and hurried down the drive behind the cars, arriving as Ibrahim's guard, as she thought of them now, formed around him.

'Sorry I'm such a mess—we had quite a storm last night—and Mum's down in the bottom paddock,' she said, aware she didn't sound the least bit sorry. 'If you want to wait inside I'll get her for you.'

Ibrahim waved away her apology and her offer.

'It is you I have come to see.' He spoke so formally Kate felt a whisper of apprehension slither down her spine. Studying him more closely, it seemed he'd aged since the previous day—grown weaker in some way. Shock over the bee-sting incident, or was the man not well? Could she enquire about his health, or would that be breaking some protocol she didn't understand?

'Let's sit on the deck,' she suggested, deciding to keep an eye on him as they spoke. Maybe an opening would arise when she could ask him if he was all right.

Having decided this, she led him around the side of the house to the wide, paved deck that looked down towards the river. 'These chairs are used to work clothes.'

To Kate's surprise, only Ibrahim followed her; the other men remained by the cars, although the one who'd attended her father's funeral had peeled off from the group and was heading for the stables.

'Why—?' she began.

'He will find your mother and talk with her,' Ibrahim said, his smile allaying a little of her tension. 'You must not be alarmed.'

Kate found herself smiling right back. There was

something about this man—the mix of old-world charm and courtly manners—that made her feel safe.

Safe from what?

She had no idea.

She led him up onto the terrace and waved him into a chair, then wondered about the propriety of offering a wet chair to a sultan.

'I think they're all dry but you'd better check,' she said. 'Sometimes a storm blows rain in under the roof.'

Ibrahim obediently felt his chair before sitting down, but now, seated herself, the safe feeling had gone and Kate was feeling *more* than a whisper of apprehension.

Had he decided it was easier to tell her rather than her mother that he wasn't buying Tippy?

What else could it be?

She was about to offer tea or coffee so she could get away for a few minutes and calm herself when he spoke.

'Firstly, I wish to thank you for what you did. Dr McLean tells me you saved Fareed's life and I am grateful, as would be my family and all my people for he is greatly loved. So here is where we are. I will buy your mother's horse, not out of gratitude but because I agree with my stud master that Dancing Tiptoe is a magnificent animal and will hopefully become a great racehorse.'

Kate's heart sank.

Stupid, really, when the sale meant her mother's breeding business would survive, and no doubt prosper, once word got around. But it was the training that her mother loved and to lose a horse with Tippy's potential…

Was she thinking this to stop herself thinking about Billy?

About what losing Tippy would do to Billy's fragile health?

His happiness?

Tippy was his life!

Ibrahim was still talking—she *had* to listen. Later she'd worry about Billy. He was saying…

Saying he'd leave the horse with her mother?

'You'd let her train him? Not take him away? Oh, thank you, Ibrahim, you have no idea how much that would mean to her.'

'And to your brother?'

Kate nodded.

'Yes, Billy and Tippy have been inseparable since

Tippy was a foal. Billy has some kind of special bond with all the horses, but with Tippy it is so much more—as if he's found a soul mate.'

'I guessed as much,' Ibrahim said quietly, 'but, as I said earlier, there is a bargain attached. We love bargaining, we of ancient desert blood.'

Ah, the catch, Kate thought, tension building within her as she waited for the axe to drop on this dream result.

'I know our ways are different but they have proved successful over thousands of years. For a long time now I have been looking for a wife for my nephew, and in you I believe I have found a person of strength and character who would be a perfect match for him.'

'I'm sorry? You want me to marry a total stranger because you think we'd be a perfect match? Ibrahim, I don't want to be rude, but that's ridiculous!'

Far from being offended, Ibrahim smiled calmly and continued as if she'd never spoken.

'I would not hold you to the marriage if, after a certain time, you both felt it was untenable, but I would like you to give it time, say a year. I realise this must seem strange to you—'

'Strange? It's beyond strange. Bizarre might come near but—'

She wasn't allowed to finish—not that she could think past the 'but'.

'To us it is a normal arrangement,' her guest said. 'You will have much in common, for you are both doctors and I believe your recent work has been in Emergency, which is where my nephew works in a new hospital purpose-built for such things. So you could work together, although, of course, you would not have to work unless you wished to.'

He had it all planned out, and he spoke as if this was a rational, reasonable conversation.

Which, of course, it wasn't! Not rational or reasonable at all! Totally unreasonable. Ridiculous, in fact! Although somewhere in the chaos in her head she remembered where this conversation had begun.

It was a bargain.

If she did this, he would not only buy Tippy but would allow her mother to train him.

Here, at the stud…

With Billy…

'And your nephew, what does he have to say to this?' she asked, squelching the questions that she really wanted answers to—why couldn't he find his own wife? Was he a five-foot-two moron with bad skin and a stutter?

Not that a five-foot-two moron with bad skin and a stutter couldn't be a wonderful man and a great husband, but—

'Fareed will accept I am acting in his best interests.'

'Fareed?' The name came out in a disbelieving squeak. 'The man whose throat I cut? That's the man you want me to marry?'

Settle down, Kate, breathe—but before she could obey this sensible order, another thought struck her.

'This isn't like some old Chinese proverb where, if you save a person's life you're responsible for them for ever, is it? I'm a doctor, it's my job—and think of all the doctors in the world who'd be burdened down with all those responsibilities. No, Ibrahim, it's impossible.'

Ibrahim regarded her, his face grave.

'I would not put responsibility for a life on anyone,' he said. 'In my position, I am only too aware of the burden of responsibility. I understand, as a doctor, you did what you had to do and as a result Fareed is alive. But this is a separate issue.'

He paused, looking out over the home paddock to the river, his face troubled by thoughts Kate couldn't guess at.

Not that she wanted to guess at anything—she was too busy trying to order her own thoughts.

Marry a man to save her family?

It was medieval!

But if she did it…

Ibrahim was talking again, and she forced herself to listen.

'I have been seeking a suitable wife for him for some time,' he said. 'He is thirty-seven and it is time he was married. It struck me yesterday that you would be a perfect match for him. You are strong, and resourceful, and caring of your family—this last is important to me because family is who we are.'

'But that's just it—family! *My* family!' Kate pointed out. 'I've come home to help Mum here at the stud, I can't go off and leave her now. She'll have more work than ever.'

Besides which she'd kill me if she thought I'd agree to such a stupid bargain for her sake.

Or Billy's…?

Ibrahim was talking again and Kate tried to concentrate, although the confusion in her mind was making it near impossible.

'I will provide the best available help for your mother,' he said firmly. 'An overseer, stable hands, new vehicles, whatever she will need.'

No confusion now! Kate closed her eyes and saw exactly how the stables could be—the way her mother had always dreamed they'd be, although somehow her father had always managed to lose whatever money they'd had before the dream could be realised.

Her mother would be in heaven.

And Billy would have Tippy.

But her mother would be horrified at the 'bargain'.

Not if she didn't know…

That last sneaky thought hit Kate like a sharp slap.

Was she actually considering Ibrahim's mad idea? Could she really deceive her mother?

She looked at the man who sat quietly beside her, gazing out at the green fields and river gums. Not the courtly gentleman she'd met the day before but someone older, more tired, somehow.

She dragged her mind back from the man to the question.

'But surely your nephew should marry someone from your own country. Someone who would know how—well, how to behave,' she offered desperately.

Ibrahim shook his head, but now he smiled.

'I have thought hard on it, and you would be my choice. Fareed is the son of my older brother so he is also my heir, and although he will be a wise and just ruler, he has ghosts in his life, ghosts I fear will stop him reaching his full potential.'

'So I'm not only supposed to marry this man but banish his demons, as well?' Kate demanded. 'Shouldn't you be calling an exorcist?'

She knew she was being flippant, but right now flippant was all she could manage. The turmoil inside her—the feeling of being torn in two—was just too much!

Ibrahim offered her a slight smile but obviously wasn't diverted from his course.

'I would not put such a burden on you, although I believe you could be the person to help him out of the past. It is why I have chosen you. And, as I said, I would not hold you to the marriage—divorce is simple in my country and should that happen, provided I believe you have behaved honourably, I will honour my agreement with your mother. That would be our bargain.'

Bargain!

The word brought her right back to where this bizarre conversation had started. Ibrahim would buy Tippy, have her mother train him, provide an overseer and stable help and the stables would not only survive but would undoubtedly thrive.

As would Billy!

And all she, Kate, had to do, was...

Marry the man with the disdainful yet seductively attractive face?

The words roared in her head, while a tremor of what she hoped was fear and not desire stirred inside her.

She tried desperately to pull herself together—to come up with some sensible, solid, irrefutable reasoning against this ridiculous idea.

All she came up with was a question.

'I can work while I'm there?'

'Of course,' Ibrahim replied. 'We would really appreciate it if you did.'

'So you need doctors—or a doctor?'

He shook his head.

'Doctors we can buy.'

'And you can't buy wives?' The words were out before she'd thought them through, and as soon as they were hanging there, in the bright morning air, she realised her mistake.

'But, of course, that's what you're doing.'

Ibrahim studied her for a moment.

'We are traders back as far as our people go. Trade is give and take. It is bartering and making bargains, that is how we do things. You talk of buying as if it is a bribe, but if you could see it our way, maybe it would not look so ugly to you.'

'And Fareed? What does he think of this?'

Ibrahim's smile turned him back into the man she'd first met—the charming man her mother had introduced in the stables.

'He has no need to know who—it is enough that he knows he is to marry a woman I have chosen. He will meet you on his wedding night.'

'Wedding night?'

Kate's voice was back to squeaky—squeaky with disbelief.

'Our weddings are different. You will be married with the woman supporting you, and he with the men, so you will not meet until after the ceremony and feasting is over.'

It isn't that part of the 'wedding night' phrase that worries me, Kate wanted to say, but somehow it didn't seem appropriate.

Not that any of this conversation had been particularly appropriate...

CHAPTER THREE

FAREED WAS PUZZLED when the limousine sent to collect him from the hospital didn't contain his uncle, and even more surprised when the driver announced they were going straight to the airport.

'The sultan is staying on for a few days but knows you wish to get back to work,' the driver informed him. 'His plane will take you home and return for him.'

Fareed wasn't entirely surprised. After his uncle had dropped his bombshell at the hospital, the evening after his allergic reaction to the bee, Ibrahim had avoided opportunities for further conversation—opportunities he couldn't have escaped if they'd flown home together.

That conversation had been startling, to say the least—shocking, in fact. He had known for some time that his days as a bachelor were numbered. Knew also that his uncle would be choosing his bride. After all, as Ibrahim had pointed out, he'd had plenty of time to find one for himself. And it was in keeping with the tradition of the family, and their people, so there was little point in arguing about it.

But the last thing Fareed had expected his uncle to announce on his hospital visit was a date for his wedding—a date within a fortnight of their return to Amberach.

Even more disturbing was his uncle's refusal to tell him the name of his bride-to-be. It would almost certainly be some distant cousin, someone Ibrahim had been secretly grooming—or having groomed—for the job. Because that's what it was—a job, a duty, preordained almost…

No, it was perfectly understandable that Ibrahim would be avoiding him!

Had she actually agreed?

That was Kate's first thought when, three days after Ibrahim's morning visit, Isaac, the man who'd first seen Tippy, arrived at the house, bringing with him a young stableboy, several mounds of luggage and an elegant leather folder, embossed in gold, with what must be the crest of Amberach and Kate's name.

It contained not only details of the flight she

would take to Amberach with the sultan in two days' time but also coloured brochures about the country, its people and history right up to recent times, where a picture showed the sultan, in a long white robe and gold-edged headscarf, cutting the ribbon in front of the new emergency hospital.

A tall, distinguished-looking man, similarly dressed except for black edging on his headscarf, stood beside Ibrahim.

Fareed!

Kate peered at the photo—hoping to read something positive in the shadowed features?

He was as good looking as she'd first thought him, but good looks were usually way down on her list of important manly attributes.

Manly attributes?

What *was* she thinking?

'I do wish you hadn't made such a quick decision about going over there to work,' her mother said when she saw the documents, and Kate knew her mother suspected something.

Not a marriage something, that was for sure, but she knew something had gone on between Ibrahim and Kate.

'Mum, it's a brand-new hospital—look—and

I'm only going for a year. It's not as if I haven't been away before, and think how exciting it will be. Look at the brochures Ibrahim has sent. What's more, you'll be so busy with training and getting the new staff into order, you won't even notice I'm gone.'

Sally smiled.

'It *is* good for us all, isn't it? Like a gift from heaven, to be able to keep Tippy here for Billy—'

'And for you to train him, Mum, to show what you can do with a really good horse! It's time to stop dreaming and get working.'

Sally hugged her hard and Kate swallowed the lump that had formed in her throat.

This is all for Mum and Billy, she reminded herself, *and for the future of this family*—my *family*.

Twelve months of her life was a small price to pay for the happiness she was bringing these two people, whom she loved with all her heart.

And there was no way she could think beyond that—except perhaps, from a purely selfish motive, it would offer a chance to put her life back together after Mark…

'Snow-capped mountains?'

Ibrahim smiled at the disbelief in Kate's voice.

'You did not expect them?'

'I saw the pictures in the brochures, but it still seems strange to see snow in a desert.'

Her host had spent most of the flight tucked away in what he called his mobile office, catching up on business and resting when he could. Perhaps he wasn't well, the kindly Ibrahim—could this be why he was so anxious to marry off his nephew?

You don't know enough about any of it, Kate told herself. *Just be glad you had a good sleep so you can face whatever lies ahead.* She felt fresh and rested, having lazed and slept in first-class luxury until a steward had brought breakfast and opened the blind for her to see Amberach for the first time.

Ibrahim had slid into the seat beside her as she'd blurted out her surprise.

'Amberach has everything,' he explained. 'It is winter now so there is more snow, but on the highest peaks a little snow remains all year round. It is the snow melt that makes the land around the base of the mountains fertile, and has provided a good living for our farmers throughout the ages. But the fertile plain is narrow and on two sides of my country the great desert has encroached more and more—right to the coast, where many of my people have lived on fishing and pearl diving for generations.'

'Do you still have a pearling industry?' Kate asked.

'I am trying to revive it, if only as an added incentive for tourists to visit my country,' Ibrahim said, as the plane swooped lower, over dark blue sea and yellow-gold sand. 'Once cultured pearls came on the market, our pearling fleets went out of business. Most turned to fishing, but the fisherman must go farther and farther from shore to get a good catch.'

Kate nodded, remembering the things she'd read, but the plane was coming in to land and a mixture of excitement and apprehension at what lay ahead held her silent.

The plane landed but no one moved and to Kate's surprise it was then towed into a huge hangar, sumptuously decorated in deep reds and purple and gold.

'The women of the family prefer to alight in privacy,' Ibrahim explained, 'although these days many of them, especially the younger ones, frequent the shopping malls and go with friends to the theatre.'

They disembarked, Ibrahim ushering Kate into yet another sleek black vehicle—into the front seat this time.

'I have asked Fareed to meet us here. He will take you for a short drive along the esplanade and past the old fort on the way to the palace. It will be an opportunity for the two of you to talk a little but remember, he knows nothing of the wedding plans. It is not necessary for him to know until the wedding night.'

Kate frowned at the man she'd discovered was so devious and felt her stomach knot at the thought of the deception she would have to play.

Or was it deception if Fareed didn't know?

She heard voices and looked up to see him striding into the hangar.

'Is this really necessary, Uncle?' he demanded. 'Do you not have enough lackeys that one couldn't be found to show Dr Andrews around this morning? I'm barely back at work and you call me away.'

His face might be a mask, but his eyes glittered with fury.

Kate tried to blend into the car, to pretend she wasn't there at all, but Ibrahim was unrelenting.

'It is a small thing I ask of you,' he was saying to

Fareed. 'Dr Andrews is our guest and all I would wish of you is to show her a little hospitality. Perhaps as a mark of your gratitude…'

'In that great hulking limousine? If you want me to play tour guide she can ride with me in my car.'

Kate thought she detected a quick smirk on Ibrahim's face and wondered just how wide his manipulative streak might be.

'Well, come along!'

Fareed this time, the order curt.

She longed to rebel, to tell the pair of them she wasn't just a piece of meat to barter over, but she bit her tongue because, sadly, that was exactly what she was—Ibrahim's pawn.

She forced herself to think of the rewards of the position—the continued success of the family business, her mother's and Billy's happiness…

Billy! In her head she saw the tiny scrap of humanity that had been her longed-for baby brother, born twelve weeks early and looking like the living doll she'd been imagining. All tied up with wires, his little eyes taped shut, tiny hands and feet and tubes everywhere.

Billy, who'd fought to live, then battled through one illness after another to survive.

Billy, who'd only really come fully alive when Tippy had been born and the two of them had formed some magical bond.

She shut away the memories and followed meekly behind the angry man who so obviously didn't want to be stuck with her.

If he only knew...

Fareed's vehicle was a high-set SUV, black like most of the vehicles she'd seen these people use.

'Why are all the cars black?' she asked, as she clambered in, unaided by her husband-to-be.

'They aren't,' he replied—two crisp words cutting off any further conversation.

Kate studied his profile—more stern than arrogant—and shivered inside. Perhaps there was still time to pull out of this arrangement. She could speak to Ibrahim and ask if she could work for two years—even three—instead of marrying this man, but she knew she couldn't risk the happiness of the two people she loved best in all the world.

And yet if she *was* going to marry Fareed, shouldn't she at least attempt to get to know him?

'I'm sorry you were pulled away from your work. If I had known Ibrahim was going to interrupt your work to take care of me, I could have asked him to call me a cab.'

Fareed's reply was a derisive snort.

'Call a cab when he has a dozen vehicles at his disposal and probably twice as many drivers? I'm to take you to the palace where, no doubt, he'll be happy to organise a car and a driver to be put at your disposal for however long you are here.'

He turned to study her as the traffic slowed.

'It seems you have bewitched him.'

How to respond?

'Nonsense! He's asked me here as thanks for the bee episode and so I could see your country and perhaps work here for a while. I imagine, once I start work, I can live in at the hospital.'

Another snort.

Kate sighed.

If the man was like this when he thought her just a visitor, how much more awkward and dismissive would he be when he discovered she was to become his wife?

She should tell him—let him work it out with Ibrahim—but she had given her word she'd tell no one of the agreement. To all intents and purposes, she was coming here to work, full stop.

And as for seeing sights, so far all they'd seen was traffic. Was this Fareed's way of disobeying his uncle's orders? She'd have been better off being shown around by one of the camels wandering across the streets—the cause of the traffic chaos.

'Are they sacred animals that they are allowed right of way?' she asked, and Fareed, though he looked momentarily shocked that she had asked a question, did, finally, reply.

'No, just animals with minds of their own! But they have been essential to the survival of my people for thousands of years, so no one would harm one. We will be out of this traffic soon.'

Kate turned her attention back to her surroundings.

Rows of small shops and businesses gave way to signs of development, boarded lots, some with massive cranes rising behind the fences, and beyond them the outlying residential area of a sparkling new city.

'How exciting it must be to be able to build a city from scratch,' Kate said. 'To try to get it right from the beginning.'

For a moment she thought Fareed wouldn't answer, but after a swift glance her way, he relented.

'This city is my uncle's dream. He had so many

plans he needed teams of architects and engineers and builders to implement them. He drew the best from all over the world, told them what he wanted, then made sure he got it. He might appear a charming cosmopolitan man but he has the core of steel all our leaders had to keep the tribes alive in inhospitable places for thousands of years.'

Kate heard the words but also the love this man must feel for Ibrahim. Could a man who loved his uncle be all bad?

The vehicle left the city, the built and unbuilt bits of it, and swung onto a wide road that ran along the shoreline.

'Oh!'

Kate barely breathed the word, so astonished was she by the wide stretch of golden sound reaching out to the deep blue of a placid sea. Squat palm trees lined the landward side of the road and beyond them, green parklands stretched to the foothills of craggy red-grey mountains.

The road curved gently around the shallow bay, coming to a point where rugged cliffs met the sea, and perched atop the cliffs, like something formed from the land itself, there was a multi-towered building.

The old fort?

'How do you get to it?' Kate asked, staring up now at the sheer cliffs.

'There is a way from the inland side,' Fareed explained. 'And a secret way from the sea. Once it was a place of refuge for the fishermen who lived along the shore, but now it is deserted, except for the caretakers and some artisans who are restoring parts that have deteriorated.'

As they rounded the corner, Kate turned back to look again, marvelling at the beauty of the structure and wondering how on earth it had been built on such an impossible site.

But they were passing the fishing village now, the colourful boats tied up along the shore, and beyond the village high mud brick walls—

'Another fort?'

'The palace,' Fareed replied.

She was here!

In Amberach!

With her bridegroom?

CHAPTER FOUR

THE PLANS FOR the wedding were completely out of Kate's hands, and there were brief moments when she allowed herself to relax and enjoy her new surroundings, but the strain of deceiving her mother lived with her night and day.

Too afraid her mother would hear the anxiety in her voice, or that even talking to her mother—*lying* the way she was—would make her break down, Kate had used the time difference between the countries as an excuse to communicate through emails.

The pain of the deception stayed with her as she settled in the palace, in her own suite of rooms in the enormous, rambling, maze of a place.

In reality she'd had little time for worry or self-pity, with various female members of Ibrahim's family fluttering around her, helping her settle in, filling her so-called 'dressing-room' with garments and gowns she was sure she'd never wear, underwear so fine it looked as if it would fall apart if she breathed and nightgowns that made her blush.

In the bathroom she'd found perfumes, soaps, creams and various unguents she'd only sniffed at, filling an entire wall of shelves, while another cabinet carried an array of make-up from the top French cosmetic manufacturers.

The day before the wedding, she was escorted to a large reception area. It was magnificent, the floors covered in silk carpets woven in dazzling jewel colours, the walls carved with fanciful trees and flowers and painted, again in brilliant colour. Arched windows along one side of the room must look out into the big courtyard that Kate had been too timid to explore.

She only knew it was laid out in patterns similar to the carpets, with a fountain in the centre and trees and bushes cut into fantastic shapes. Not that she could see it now, for filmy silk curtains covered the windows, billowing slightly in the breeze.

Following her escorts, she was led to the far end of the room and seated on a low divan in the middle of a kind of dais, so she was raised above anyone coming into the room. Women began arriving—women she'd never met, although all of them appeared very excited to be meeting her. And all of them were beautifully dressed in designer fashions once they'd removed the black *abayas* that had covered their gowns.

They cooed and oohed and touched her clothes— a beautiful silk gown in palest lemon—and her hair—in its usual unruly plait down her back, and cooed and oohed again.

Several younger girls appeared, giggling and carrying pots of what looked like paste.

'This is your henna party,' one of them, who introduced herself as Farida, told her. 'We are to be your attendants today and tomorrow. We are cousins of Fareed. This is Suley and this is Mai.'

They set down the pots they carried, and beckoned an older woman towards them.

'Hayla is the best henna artist in the country. She will do a beautiful job. Your skin is so pale, the henna patterns will look stunning.'

Henna?

Artist?

Patterns?

Kate longed to ask for details but the girls were chattering excitedly amongst themselves and more and more women were arriving, introducing themselves and touching her, as if checking she was real.

The three handmaidens cleared everyone away, and the artist knelt in front of Kate, taking one of her feet in her hands and turning it this way and that.

She opened the lid on one of the pots and Kate realised what was happening. She'd seen pictures of women with their hands and feet decorated with the dark red-brown colour—henna.

Fascinated in spite of herself, she watched as a lacy pattern of vines and leaves began to show up on her foot. Thick heavy lines, although, as Farida explained, the thickness was there to dye the pattern into the skin and would later be washed away.

'But you must be very still,' Mai warned.

So Kate sat, looking out at the partying women, all eating now, maids circling the room with great platters of food.

And Fareed?

What would he be doing?

She pictured his face, trying to wipe off the disdain. He was certainly a handsome man, and well built—something she'd realised as she'd struggled to get him to relax after the bee sting.

But how the hell was he going to react when he realised who Ibrahim had chosen for his wife?

Fareed stalked through the hospital, his usual pleasure in the place he had created deadened by the dread of what was to occur tomorrow. The marrying part was all right—he'd known he had to marry, and soon—but he knew his uncle well enough to know the old man was plotting something—something Fareed guessed he would not enjoy.

He'd slept in his apartment at the palace the previous night, hoping to pick up some gossip about what lay ahead, but even his most devoted of servants were tight-lipped. Either that, or they, too, had been kept in the dark. He might as well return to his apartment here at the hospital tonight—one last night of freedom.

How bad could it be? he asked himself as he continued his patrol of the reception area, glaring at anyone unfortunate enough to cross his tracks. Apart from sleeping with the woman from time to time in order to produce some heirs, he need have nothing to do with her. Once the wedding month—which was, in fact, forty days—was over, she'd have her own apartment in the women's part of the palace and he need never see her, except in bed.

With the lights out!

He shuddered at the thought of having sex because it was his duty, not because he was attracted to a woman. Perhaps he wouldn't be able to perform?

He slammed a hand against his head and was glad when his pager called him to the emergency room, so he could concentrate on work to escape the wild imaginings running through his brain.

At least thinking about the wedding was distracting him from thinking about the woman who was supposed to be coming to work at the hospital— the woman with the flaming hair, at one with the horse she rode so expertly.

He knew she was staying at the palace, but as yet there'd been no mention of when she might deign to start work. He should probably have asked either her or Ibrahim but, as far as he was concerned, getting over the wedding was enough to be worrying about without having to consider a woman who, for reasons beyond his understanding, he found profoundly disturbing.

In fact, the longer she stayed away from the hospital, the happier he'd be.

Sitting still was hard, although Kate was fed tidbits by her new-found friends. Little morsels of delicious food, sips of brightly coloured fruit juices. And below her the party swirled, while beautiful women, tall and short, imperious looking or gently feminine, all clad in glorious gowns, came up onto the dais to check on the progress of the henna and to admire the patterns, most of them still touching her hair as they passed by.

'Are redheads so rare in Amberach,' she asked the girls, and they giggled behind their hands.

'Yes, but they say your colouring reminds them of Fareed's mother,' Mai added. 'Apparently, she, too, had red hair, though none of us ever saw her.'

Uh-oh! Kate thought as things began to click into place. Was this why Ibrahim had chosen her? Was Fareed's mother one of the ghosts he carried in his head? And, if so, what was she, Kate, supposed to do about it?

Icy dread crept through her veins. The moment he realised just who his bride was, Fareed would know just how badly Ibrahim had treated him—had tricked him.

And her!

She needed to know more about Fareed's family—his parents—and what had happened to them, but even after such a short stay in Amberach, she knew she couldn't ask. Questions about families were taboo.

Although she *could* ask Ibrahim!

With two feet and one hand painted?

No, she couldn't stop this process now, but she needed to speak to Ibrahim—to demand to know if he'd chosen her because she bore some curious resemblance to Fareed's mother.

She'd tell him…

What?

That she couldn't be part of a plan to deliberately hurt Fareed?

That she couldn't go through with the wedding?

And tell her mother and Billy what, when she returned home and Tippy was sent to another trainer?

She breathed deeply, hoping to calm her racing thoughts, but the coldness remained in her body, although in her heart she felt a spark of pity for the man she was pledged to marry.

* * *

The morning of the wedding arrived. Kate woke and stared in fascination at the intricate patterns decorating her hands and feet. The henna paste had been put on thickly and allowed to stay there for many hours before being washed off to leave the delicate pattern behind it.

The women she couldn't help thinking of as her handmaidens appeared in a welter of excitement, each bearing articles of clothing that appeared to be made out of spun gold. They shouted orders at the two servants, Mariam and Layla, who would appear from nowhere whenever Kate came to her room or woke from sleep.

'Cloth of gold out of one of the treasure chests, no doubt,' Kate muttered at Mariam, whom, she knew, spoke no English. Mariam was trying to re-move Kate's pyjamas—old favourites she'd brought from home and refused to be parted from.

Dodging the ministrations of her helper, she grabbed Layla, whom she knew *did* speak English, and told her she would dress herself.

'But you must bathe, and be made up, and prop-erly dressed from the skin out, for he will want to unwrap you like a precious parcel.'

The excitement in Layla's voice suggested this was the most momentous moment in a woman's life.

There'll be no unwrapping of this parcel, Kate told herself, although this time silently because making a mockery of the wedding in front of these women would be unkind, and probably go against her part of the bargain.

She and Fareed would sort out what happened after the wedding, and whatever they decided would be their business. And in spite of her nerves, she was fairly certain she could reach some arrangement with him—after all, she was probably the last woman on earth *he'd* want to marry. This was not an affair of the heart but a business arrangement and she could—she would—make it work.

So she went along with being bathed in water with rose petals floating in it, in being massaged with cream that made her skin feel like silk and being dressed in golden knickers and a golden bra, a long golden underskirt and a huge, all-encompassing golden gown on top of it all.

As if this was not enough, a golden shawl was draped across her hair, and a fine gold veil drawn down across her face.

At least she thought it was her face, although it, too, had been painted, her eyes outlined in thick, dark kohl, her eyebrows extended, so from behind the veil all that could be seen were dark, mysterious eyes.

Behind her geeky spectacles that she'd deliberately chosen after losing so many smaller, fashionable pairs, or broken them by sitting on them, or mutilated them in a dozen different ways.

'You *cannot* wear them,' Farida decreed, seizing them from Kate's hand and secreting them in a pocket in her gown. 'It spoils the whole look.'

'But I can't see where I'm going without them,' Kate protested.

The young women laughed.

'We are to escort you to your throne and you won't have to move from there until the party is over and the prince comes to claim his bride. Then he will guide you to the marriage chamber.'

'Marriage chamber?'

Kate's voice faltered over the words and the women laughed again, making jokes in their own language and dissolving into hilarity.

Think of it as part of the job, she told herself, *and just go along with it.*

She was led into a room full of women, maybe four hundred of them, with more coming in all the time. From her seat back on the dais she could see they entered with their black *abayas* covering their clothes, with evening scarves, although it was only mid-morning, covering their hair. Evening scarves, she'd learned, could be coloured and patterned and embroidered with bright thread and studded with jewels.

Even without her glasses, she realised the women were no sooner safe inside the room—a women's place—than they stripped off scarves and long black cloaks, revealing themselves in the brightest of gowns, floor-length ballgowns mostly, their necks and arms adorned with brilliant jewellery.

It was a stunning mosaic of colour, swirling below her, voices rising higher and higher as friends and relatives greeted each other.

Farida, Suley and Mai stayed with her, lying against cushions near her feet, taking plates of food from the servants to offer her a taste of this or that, pouring cardamom-scented coffee for her.

But although she'd seen the local women eat and even drink behind their veils she had no idea how they did it, and, terrified of spilling something on the beautiful clothes, she did nothing more than sip a little water now and then.

From time to time she was conscious of a noise from outside the room.

'It's the men's party,' Suley explained. 'They chant as they do the old dances, and sing songs of the victories their tribes won many years ago.'

Would Fareed be dancing and singing?

Conjuring up his face, she doubted it. He didn't look like a man who'd give himself up to gaiety.

The day wore on, the women dancing now, their scarves tied around their hips to accentuate the movements of the dances. They danced alone, sometimes falling back to watch one person perform then joining in again so now it was a kaleidoscope of colour swirling in front of Kate as she sat and waited for what lay ahead.

Dreading it—not the marriage part, since surely in this day and age, two adults could sort that out— but Fareed's reaction to his uncle's choice…to her.

Finally a man appeared at one end of the room— a tall man, robed, like she was, but in pure white, with golden braid around the neck and sleeves, and a golden cord holding his headscarf in place.

A sudden hiatus in her heartbeats told her it was

Fareed, although he was still too far away to recognise without her glasses.

Fareed had sat in solitary splendour on his dais
in the men's room, while the celebrations of his
wedding seethed below him. It was only when the
dancing started that he was compelled to join in,
linking arms with his uncle and one of many male
cousins in the dance of the swords.

Why the dance of the swords was performed at
weddings he had no idea, but he did know it was
near the end of the celebrations. Soon his friends
and relations would push him towards the women's
room next door. He would have to pretend to strug-
gle as he was thrust into the room full of women,
most of whom would be struggling to pull their
abayas over their fine clothes and cover their heads
before he happened to see their hair.

He would have to walk through the crush, being
examined as a fine camel was examined at the big
sales, everything but his teeth checked out, mostly
by strangers.

Once inside the room, he could see, at the far
end, three young cousins on the dais with his gold-
wrapped bride. At most of the weddings he'd at-

tended recently, the bride had opted for western bridal gear—huge marshmallow-like white gowns with white veils covering their hair and faces.

But, probably due to Ibrahim's influence, this bride was a traditional 'parcel'—a blob of gold he was expected to unwrap, presumably with pleasure and excitement.

He felt neither, and for some unknown reason his mind threw up an image of the girl on the horse, back in the green valley in Australia. It must have been the freedom of the way she'd ridden that had made the image appear now, when he was about to lose his own freedom—or a greater part of it…

He stalked down the room, the women forming a passage for him, clustering closer, seemingly looking him over—judging him—until he reached the dais on which the mystery woman sat, hidden in the folds of gold.

His young cousins helped her stand, and as he drew close they handed her to him—just like a parcel, only one with legs. He took her hennaed hand, and led her through a curtain at the back of the room, the women whooping and hollering behind them.

Wedding night!

The two words were echoing in Kate's head as he drew her down a corridor she didn't know—well, thought she didn't know, from what she could see without glasses and from behind the veil.

And into a room dominated by a humungous bed with a pure white silk coverlet, piled with pillows in the same white silk.

He let go her hand and turned towards her, saying something in his own language, talking, talking, asking something, she was sure.

She wished she could see his face more clearly but it was impossible, so she took a deep breath and spoke herself.

'Please, speak English. It's me, Kate... I thought Ibrahim would have told you.'

She was trying to untangle the veil and scarf as she spoke, so he could see as well as hear her, but it had been pinned in such a way that she was only making things worse.

She was about to ask him to help when she realised he'd stepped back as if he'd been shot.

In revulsion?

'Look, if you'd stop standing there like a dummy and help me out of this gear, I can explain everything.'

He moved, but not to help her. Instead, he turned away, pacing the room so through the golden veil he was a blur of white, stopping suddenly by the bed and ripping off his headdress, flinging it on the bed, stripping off his long cloak, his actions violent enough for Kate to make them out from behind her veil.

Then he paced again, bare chested now, with nothing but a long white piece of material covering his lower body. Barely covering, for even through the blur of gold silk she could see the flash of long tanned legs appearing and disappearing.

Totally disconcerted, and increasingly angry, she moved towards him.

'Will you stop the pacing and help me out of this get-up? And see if you can find what Farida did with my glasses? And then we could talk this through. Do you honestly believe I'd allow myself to be married to a total stranger if I didn't have a very good reason?'

'Money!'

Fareed spat the word at her, his fury so great he daren't go near her for fear he'd do her harm, preferably by strangling her so she'd shut up while he tried to think.

'Could you at least let me try to explain?' she was saying. 'Mind you, if you don't get me out of this tangle of veils I'm going to faint and, much as it might give your ego a boost to have your bride lying prostrate at your feet, I'd prefer to remain conscious.'

His ego?

What was she on about?

Surely she didn't think he had any intention of consummating this farcical marriage?

'Are you going to help or not, because if you're not I'm heading straight out the door—if I can find it—and I'm going to yell until someone does help.'

And have the whole palace know his bride had fled, screaming, from his bed? He'd be a laughing-stock—a joke—but surely that's what this was—a joke…

Ibrahim's joke!

She was stumbling in what she must have thought was the direction of the door when he caught her shoulders and spun her to face him.

Through the thin gauze covering her face he saw the kohl lining the pale green eyes he'd seen before in such a different context. Huge eyes looking up at him, a mix of fear and defiance in their depths.

And he could see this through the veil? his cynical self demanded.

But somewhere under there would be that hair—'golden' his mother had insisted he call the colour—because his uncle had played the ultimate deception. Not only had he married his nephew to a westerner but to a pale, mouthy parody of his mother.

Rage at this deception burning through his body, he ripped at the cloth that hid the woman so completely. Ignoring the look of shock on her suddenly revealed face, he tore off the outer cloak, hearing whatever hooks held it together rip from their anchors.

'Stop right now!'

Her voice was strong, though he was sure he detected a tremor of fear beneath the strength.

And well she might fear him, the barbarian inside him whispered.

But hadn't that barbarian been banished generations ago?

Maybe not, for his hands still held the cloth of gold, ready to rend it further—ready to render her naked.

'Fareed!' she said, her voice steady now, the green

eyes hazy—desperate—as she looked directly into his. 'I know you must be angry, but we can sort this out. We're both mature adults—we can talk, work out a plan. Your uncle promised it did not have to be forever, nor did he say the marriage had to be consummated. I thought we could sort out some sensible living arrangements, preferably away from the palace, and work together as colleagues. Our private life is no one else's business.'

He stared at the half-naked woman in front of him, her milk-white skin reddened in places where he'd ripped cloth across it, flimsy strips of lacy gold underwear visible through the wreckage.

Was it because it was his wedding night that the sight of that underwear against the pale skin had his groin stirring, hardening?

He spun away from the sight of her. He was angry at his uncle's deception, but even more angry now with this woman who assumed she could take control of the situation, and was suggesting some half-baked plan for them moving forward from here.

Who the hell did she think she was, planning *his* future?

And how the hell could his body possibly have

reacted to the sight of her? She was nothing more than a whore, just as his mother had been.

Kate could see the tension in his shoulders—anger, she guessed—and read disgust in his eyes as they scorched across her.

Who could blame him?

But somehow she had to make this work—to talk this man down from his anger, to sort out some arrangement he could live with, because if she failed, then all her hopes for Billy's future happiness—for her mother's future, too—would be lost.

So she had to reason with him, but not beg or plead. She knew instinctively that should she show a smidgen of weakness before this man he'd walk all over her.

'I'm sorry,' she said, trying to project calm, mature composure, while inside she felt more like unset jelly. 'I'm sure you were looking forward to what lay ahead—undoubtedly the opportunity to deflower whatever beautiful young virgin your uncle had chosen for you—and suddenly you're stuck with an ageing redhead that no number of fairy godmothers could turn into a beautiful princess. But it's only for a year. Can't we make it work?'

Had her voice wavered on that final plea so that he turned back towards her? No, it must have been her jibe about deflowering because fury flared from his eyes, as vivid as flames from a flamethrower.

'Why?' he demanded, a threat as deep as the ocean clear in his voice. 'Why should I even *try* to make it work? So you can squeeze more money from my uncle? Has he not already paid you well? I know all about greed—it is what kept my mother coming back—not me, or my father, but plain, simple greed.'

He took another turn around the room, while Kate tried to understand, not the words but the pain in his voice, but before she could feel too sorry for him he hit again with a new jibe.

'Well, go right ahead. Stretch out your grasping hands. He won't miss it, he has plenty, just don't expect me to play along with your little game. Am I supposed to get you pregnant, too? Provide him with another heir of mixed blood? Is that his little game?'

The disdain she'd first seen in his eyes back at the farm was replaced by disgust, and she wanted to cringe and fold the torn material of her gown around her, but she had her pride.

'I won't dignify that remark with a reply.'

'No?' He shot the word at her. 'You're only too happy to talk about me deflowering virgins but when I bring up a bit of reality you cringe!'

He stepped towards her and it was all she could do *not* to cringe. Instead, she straightened and looked him straight in the eye—blurrily.

'Will you just get over yourself? Okay, so you feel your uncle has cheated you—I agree. You should have been told—in fact, you should have been able to choose your own wife—but apparently things are done differently here and your uncle assured me that you were happy for him to do the choosing, so live with it.'

He stood before her so still she wondered if he was breathing. So close, she could feel the heat of his body, see, even without her glasses, the taut muscles beneath the tanned skin of his chest, the breadth of his bare shoulders, the power of his muscled arms.

The tension that had accompanied her through the day intensified to the extent she could barely breathe herself, but she *had* to sort this out.

She would *not* burst into tears of frustration, neither could she show any sign of weakness in front of this man, for although she knew so little about him she did know that if she gave ground now he'd walk all over her and the whole situation would be lost.

Dragging air into her lungs, she tried again. Not moving back from him, though his presence—less than an arm's length away—had her nerves on fire, and was sending wayward messages through her body.

'We do not have to make it work as a conventional marriage,' she said, and inwardly marvelled that she could sound so calm. 'Surely we can treat it as a professional association. I'm a good doctor who's specialised in ER work, and you need ER doctors in your new hospital. Your private life can remain your own business. There must be accommodation at the hospital we can use to get us away from the gossiping tongues of the palace. We wouldn't need to see each other away from work— even at work if you can arrange the shifts so ours don't coincide. Would that be so very difficult?'

Fareed found himself frowning at this little bit of a woman, standing so upright in front of him, refusing to back away from his anger, pale as milk, eyes huge as she tried to see without her glasses, hair like fire in the desert, asking but not pleading for his co-operation.

From her side, it *had* to be money that had made her agree to the marriage, and, heaven knew, both he and his uncle had plenty, but why had his uncle *done* this?

Why had he chosen this particular woman?

This *red-headed* woman?

What deep game was *he* playing?

And how would he, Fareed, find out if he didn't play along, at least for a short time?

He must have been staring at her for too long for suddenly he realised the skin above her barely there brassiere was reddening.

Yet still she held her ground—her pride too strong to allow her to gather the bits of torn cloth around her.

And it suddenly occurred to him that not at any time in her pleas for him to keep up this pretence of marriage had she mentioned that he owed her— owed her his life, in fact.

He knew his frown would have deepened, yet still she stood, flushed white skin burned in places by his rage, other parts teasingly covered by scraps of golden cloth.

And the green eyes, huge and looking strangely lost…

'Get some clothes on. I'll find your glasses,' he said, turning away before she saw the effect she was having on his body. 'Is there anything else you need?'

To his surprise, she smiled, pale pink lips parting to reveal small, even, white teeth, like little pearls.

Somewhere inside his head he heard the groan from the cliché he'd just used, but the description had sprung to mind, possibly to divert him from thinking of those pearly teeth nibbling at his lips, his skin…

'Some food would be good,' she said. 'I was too terrified of spilling something on the clothes to eat anything earlier.'

Which made him frown yet again as he went to the door to order food and send someone in search of her glasses. Most women he knew might have refrained from eating because they refused to allow a square inch of fat to mar their beautiful bodies, but none would have admitted it and asked for food.

When he returned, with her glasses, she was sitting on a chair by the great arched window, wrapped in a voluminous towelling robe that would have been in the bathroom.

'I've no idea where my clothes are, or even where I am in the palace,' she said, as she slid the unattractive spectacles into place. 'When I arrived I had some rooms that led out onto a terrace and then into the garden, but I can't see anything but darkness from here.'

He felt behind the ornate Persian rug that decorated the wall beside the window and flicked a switch.

'Oh!'

The word was barely breathed, and when she turned towards him he couldn't help but read the wonder of what she was seeing in her eyes.

'But it's so beautiful,' she whispered. 'Like something from another time.'

'And you want us to go and live in a hospital apartment? They're much the same here as they are all over the world.'

'Of course they'd be the same, but we can't stay here,' she said, turning back to take in the beauty beyond the window once again.

He was looking at her looking out, looking at the long plait of red-gold hair lying against the white robe, hearing something a little like regret in her voice.

'Why not?' someone said, and he was reasonably sure it had been him.

Kate wrapped the robe more tightly around her body and stared out at the small courtyard beyond the window. Stairs from a wide terrace, overhung with vines of some kind, led down to a small swimming pool set in a garden of palms and flowering rose bushes.

Tucked in one corner was a small cabana with what looked like a spa beneath it and at the other end of the courtyard a small pergola. But it was the way the area was set out, like a pattern on one of the beautiful silk carpets that abounded in the palace, that had stolen her breath.

'My father had it built for my mother. It is completely private and the only access is through this suite of rooms, so you can use it at any time.'

She turned, looking up at Fareed, who stood behind her.

'Like now?'

He frowned but nodded, and because she was beginning to believe this was one of his few facial expressions—disdain, disgust and frown—the frown didn't bother her.

She'd kept the bra and knickers on under the robe; she could swim in them. Surely a quick swim would clear her head.

'How do I get out there?'

Still frowning he showed her how the window was really a huge arched door, and even opened it for her.

Still in the robe, she slipped out into the rose-scented air, across the terrace, down the steps, dropping the robe and her glasses by the edge of the pool and diving in.

Fareed watched her swim up and back, her white arms drawing her slim body through the water with surprising speed, turning and swimming again, back and forth in the small pool.

In all the times he'd been brought to visit his mother in this suite of rooms he'd never seen her venture into the courtyard, let alone swim, so the sight of the night swimmer held him transfixed.

A knock on the door told him the food he'd ordered had arrived and he quickly gathered up the torn material of his bride's gown and shoved it into the bathroom before opening the door. Palace servants had eyes like falcons and few were loyal enough to keep all they saw to themselves.

The young woman who entered set the tray on the table, bowed slightly and departed, her bare feet shuffling across the carpet the only sound in the silent room.

He opened the door and stepped outside, intending to call the woman—Kate, Katya in the marriage ceremony. But beneath the vines that overhung the terrace was a small table and two chairs and a sudden impulse made him carry the tray of food outside.

'Here is food,' he said, loudly enough for her to break her stroke, looking up at him with strands of her darkened hair clinging to her face and neck.

He should have turned away immediately, but couldn't, transfixed by the ease with which she pulled herself free of the water, rising almost straight out of it, like a mermaid from the depths.

Gold lace clung to her breasts—full but not too full—and hid her womanhood, but the shape of that white body, the slim waist, and rounded hips…

He turned way, more angry than ashamed, angry at the betrayal of his body.

'Aren't you hungry? Don't you want some food?'

she called, and by the time he faced her she was once again enveloped in the too-big robe and was bent over, wringing water from her long plait.

Stupid, stupid, stupid, Kate! What had prompted her to ask that question? Why hadn't she kept her mouth shut and let him disappear to wherever he'd intended disappearing to?

She glanced up and saw he was standing by the table, as if uncertain she'd actually asked him to share the snack.

'Well, sit, why don't you,' she muttered at him as she came up the shallow steps. 'We're both adults, surely we can handle this.'

'I can handle it better when you've got clothes on,' he said, and the statement was so totally un-expected that Kate *had* to laugh.

'I won't take it as a compliment,' she said, still smiling. 'After all, it's a perfectly natural reaction for men to feel some kind of hormonal reaction to naked females, like dogs do to bitches in heat.'

CHAPTER FIVE

HE SAT—HEAVEN only knew why, except he *was* hungry. He'd been too busy accepting congratulations—that was a joke—to eat much during the partying.

Kate—his wife—was studying the food rather cautiously, finally settling on a slice of melon that would do little to alleviate her hunger.

'Do you know what it all is?' he asked, mainly to divert himself from noticing the way delicate tendrils of hair were drying on her forehead and those teeth biting into the melon.

She glanced up at him.

'Some of it, although people have been very kind and mostly asking what I'd like to eat so I've stuck with things I know, like rice and fruit and vegetables.'

He felt a twinge of sympathy for her, quickly dismissed when he reminded himself she'd chosen to come here—to accept his uncle's bribe.

But she was right, they were both adults—they just had to work out a way out of this tangle. If he found out how much she expected from his uncle, he could offer her more to leave.

Now!

Well, soon...

So play nice!

He took a small china bowl and spooned rice into it, then added two little kofta and some nutty sauce.

'Try this,' he said, passing it to her, unable to stop himself noticing how small her hands were, with fine, delicate fingers, enhanced by the patterns of henna and tipped with pink, unvarnished nails. 'The kofta are little meatballs usually made with lamb or goat. In old times they could just as easily have been camel meat, although that was more usually used in dishes where the meat was cut into pieces and cooked over the fire for a long time.'

She waited politely until he'd finished speaking, then she dipped a little kofta into the sauce and ate it, nodding her appreciation and finishing the bowl.

'Oh, that was good, I'd like to have some more but I must try the other things first. That looks like eggplant.'

He gave its local name and spooned some into another dish, together with a mix of beans and spices that was his favourite.

She ate that as happily as she had the first dish, although she did pause halfway through.

'You're not eating?'

He could hardly tell her he'd been too busy studying the way *she* ate—with such enjoyment and delight. Poor woman must have been starving.

Poor woman indeed! Keep your mind on the job ahead! On the plan!

What plan?

Bribe her to go away?

He filled a bowl and began to eat, as she ventured to refill her own bowl with bits and pieces off the tray, pausing before she began on the mixture to say, 'Tell me about the hospital.'

He kept eating, surprised to find he'd be happy to talk about the hospital. He'd checked her out on the internet after her heroics at the horse stud and discovered she'd worked in some of the world's best emergency rooms, including a hospital in the US that had been the model for the one he'd set up—a hospital built primarily for emergency care.

'You worked at Goldsmith?'

Surprise flickered in her eyes.

'Internet, huh?'

'Well, we did have a fairly dramatic introduction.'

She put down her plate and studied him as he spoke.

'You would know Goldsmith was built as a purely ER hospital to divert emergency cases away from the bigger, mostly specialised, hospitals in the area—kind of like a triage hospital where patients were attended to and sent home or stabilised and sent to whichever hospital they needed.'

'Exactly.' She was nibbling on another piece of melon, tiny bites—small pearly teeth sinking into the creamy flesh...

Focus!

'We don't have big specialised hospitals, but the main hospital in town can handle most things. The problem was—' *keep your mind on work and you won't watch the teeth* '—that many of our people were intimidated by the size of the place, and they also felt that it was too—too important, if you can understand that—for them to visit with something trifling like a cut thumb, even if the thumb was hanging on by a thread.'

To his surprise she grinned at him.

'I do wish more people felt that way,' she said.

'Not the thumb hanging from a bit of skin but the people with the aches and pains who are lonely and just need someone to talk to. The good thing about Goldsmith was that we had people they *could* talk to, and psychologists to see the women who'd pop in to get a script for diazepam because they were stressed over their work, or kids, or husband, or whatever. Those people need more attention than we could ever give them in the hectic rush of a normal ER.'

The warmth in her voice and the faint flush on her cheeks told him even more than the words. This was a woman who not only enjoyed her work but understood what he wanted in *his* hospital—she'd be ideal.

That, of course, would have been in his devious uncle's head as he'd made this absurd plan. Fareed had complained to him too often about the difficulty in getting good staff—staff who cared.

Kate decided she'd look extremely greedy if she ate another piece of melon, but she had to do something because somehow she'd killed the conversation dead. Just when she was thinking maybe they *could* work out a way to survive a year of marriage, he'd cut himself off again.

All she could do was try again.

'The hospital?'

She'd barely said the words when a jangling from the bedroom behind them alerted them to a phone ringing somewhere.

'Mine,' he said, and stood up, striding back into the room.

Not knowing what to do with the tray of food, Kate left it there and followed, and once inside couldn't avoid hearing Fareed's end of the conversation, the questions he was firing into the phone making it obvious there was an emergency of some kind at the hospital.

Damn it all, her clothes had to be *somewhere*! If she went with him to the hospital to help out, proved herself as a doctor, it might put some of his aggravation to rest.

Still talking, he strode towards the wall at the end of the bed and pressed something that made a door appear. Hurrying after him, she tripped on the robe and fell into his back, all but knocking him flying, as well.

Somehow he turned and caught her, looking down into her flushed face.

'Chasing me into my dressing room?' he said, his

voice lighter than she'd ever heard—almost teasingly light. 'I thought you said we didn't need to consummate this marriage.'

She fought the blush she knew was imminent and pushed herself away.

'If this is your dressing room, where's mine? Is there a problem at the hospital? I'll get dressed and come, too—there'll be *something* I can do to help.'

She was watching his face so saw the shadows of indecision and read them easily. An extra doctor would obviously be good, but her? If he'd checked her out on the internet it couldn't be he didn't trust her as a doctor, so was it because she was a woman he didn't want her there—or because she was his wife?

He nodded as if he'd come to a decision, although reluctantly, she guessed.

'On the other side of the bed there's a rose carved on the edge of the panelling. Give it a twist and the door will slide open.'

'Slept in the bridal bed before, have you?' she teased, and was answered with a glower—a much more recognisable expression on his face.

'You've got five minutes!' he growled, and she

fled, knowing he'd leave without her if she wasn't ready.

Knowing also that she'd somehow snapped the slender thread of understanding they'd achieved as they'd talked about the hospital.

It had been her crack about the bridal suite—

Forget it and get ready!

Fortunately, all the clothes she'd brought with her when she'd come to Amberach had been moved into this room, in addition to the outfits she'd been given, which she thought of as costumes.

Pulling on jeans and a shirt over her damp underwear, she found a pair of sneakers, failed to find her socks, so put them on without. If she got blisters, she got blisters. What was a blister or two against showing this man she was as good a doctor as he was and as such should be treated with respect?

She was waiting by the door when he came out of his dressing room, dressed much the same as she was. Apparently her attire, or maybe her punctuality, met with his approval for he nodded briefly then led her through the maze of corridors to a rear entrance near the garages where a real fleet—more like forty-four than four—of vehicles was kept.

He opened the passenger door of the big black

SUV and actually put a hand under her elbow to help her in. Her skin's reaction to the touch shocked her, and much as she tried to put it down to surprise that he'd be so polite she couldn't quite believe that excuse.

Being attracted to her husband would be a totally unnecessary complication, she told herself firmly as she strapped herself in. And wasn't she right off men after Mark?

But she couldn't help but watch as he strode with swift grace around the bonnet, then swung himself in beside her in one lithe, easy movement.

It had to be the wedding thing that sent a tiny shock along her nerves as once again they were in a car together.

'You knew about the wedding plans the day I drove you from the airport,' he said suddenly.

'I did, but I'd been instructed not to mention it to you.'

Kate squirmed with embarrassment as she admitted this, but Fareed's answer was a shout of laughter.

'Smart Ibrahim! He thought of everything. Swore you to secrecy then insisted I drive you to the palace. It is custom, you see, for the bride and groom to meet briefly before the wedding. In that way he acknowledged the custom without actually letting on what he was doing.'

He paused, turning to Kate.

'You didn't feel obliged to tell me?'

No laughter in his voice now, only a hard, keen edge.

'I believed I should. I felt most uncomfortable about it, in fact, but I'd given my word to Ibrahim—'

'And you didn't want to risk losing his largesse!'

I don't care that he thinks I'm a money-hungry bitch, Kate told herself, but his words, and the way he'd said them, cut deeply into her heart.

Desperate to change the subject, she turned the conversation.

'Where are we going?'

Would he reply?

She held her breath, only releasing it when he said, 'It's an accident in the mountains.'

'The snow-capped mountains? I saw them as we flew in.'

'Not those, but closer and still rugged mountains!' He was driving fast but competently—competently enough to take his eyes off the road and glance her way. 'Did you learn anything of my country before you came? Or since you've been here? Does it interest you at all?'

The disdain she'd seen too often in his eyes was now clear in his voice, and, tired of all the antagonism between them, Kate snapped.

'I had five days before I left home to sort out the work I'd been doing for Mum, update my passport and get a visa for Amberach, let Goldsmith know I wouldn't be back for a while, get some clothes together and reassure my brother I wouldn't be eaten by bears or any other wild animal that might live here.'

She paused for breath but wasn't finished.

'But, yes, I did read brochures Ibrahim provided, although reading about a place is not the same as seeing. And apart from the drive from the airport, since I've been here I've been immured in the palace with women who want to clothe me in ball gowns and silks and satins and paint my feet and hands and face and fuss over me to absolute distraction. Then I had to practise for the wedding, which, as it turned out, was to walk onto a dais and sit there like a big parcel for a day, while women all around me danced and sang and ate.'

Much to his surprise, Fareed felt a momentary sympathy for the woman, but quickly reminded himself she'd asked for whatever treatment she'd received. Although it was a pity she hadn't seen much of his beautiful country given he had every intention of sending her home as soon as possible.

'Tell me where we're going. What's happened in these mountains of yours? Oh!'

Her cry was so genuine he turned to look at her, and saw her staring out the window. They were beyond the range of city lights now, and in the moonlight the dunes of the desert rolled out in front of them, a sea of sand with ghostly shadows chasing down the hollows and shimmering highlights on the tops, where wind had carved shapes worthy of a Michelangelo.

'It's the desert!' The genuine awe and wonder in her voice made him warm to her again. Although surely anyone, he reminded himself, who wasn't soul dead would react the same way.

Her face was alight as she looked from side to side, peering out the window and windscreen as if to take it all in at once, then abruptly they were at the mountains—at the foot of the jagged range that rose from the desert plains so suddenly that you could have been in a different country.

The road wound steeply upward, hairpin bends testing the skill of any driver. She clung to the seat but still looked out, and up now, peering around as if she could absorb it all through her skin.

A vibrant, fascinated woman!

Fascinating, as well?

He slammed the thought back into whatever dark corner it had emerged from. The small bus, carrying tourists back from a visit to the old fort, had slid off on one of the deadliest curves on the road, and the flashing lights of ambulances ahead told him they were nearly there.

'I have begun to train some of our ambulance people as paramedics—not me personally but through an excellent tutor from England. But as yet, none have finished the course, although all have done their basic first-aid training required to work as attendants.'

He pulled up out of the way of the emergency vehicles, and Kate slid out.

'Tell me what you want me to do,' she said.

'I believe they've all been rescued from the vehicle as there were fears it would either burst into flames or go crashing into the ravine below, but the attendants have done little beyond the initial ABCs.'

Airways, breathing, circulation—the beginning of any emergency treatment.

'So, will you stabilise the worst cases and send them straight to hospital?' Kate asked.

They were striding towards the well-lit scene, where uniformed attendants mingled with battered, bewildered survivors—the walking wounded.

'We'll stabilise, as in stopping bleeding or giving CPR if it's necessary. The ambulance attendants will have hooked those in need up to oxygen. It's just a matter of checking and prioritising so those in most need get first use of the ambulance.'

'Basic triage?'

'Yes,' he said. 'If you could do the first check and call me to anyone with life-threatening injuries then I'll deal with him and send him on.' He hesitated before adding, 'That sounded bad, didn't it? As if I didn't trust you? But I believe it's the most efficient use of our time.'

They paused, taking in the scene, and Kate watched him as he spoke and thought she'd surprised what could almost have been a smile out of him as he'd made the apology.

Or it could have been an optical illusion.

She rather hoped so, because as he strode ahead of her again she realised she could find a smiling Fareed quite attractive.

Quite attractive?

He'd reached the first attendant and taken a sheaf of paper and a pen from the man.

'Jot down what you find and tuck it in the patient's shirt,' he said, passing her the paper. 'The attendants all speak English, so get them to help with the lesser injured until we have transport available.'

He walked off again while Kate took a pair of gloves from an attendant and knelt beside the first patient, a small man of Eastern appearance, grey of face, his leg twisted at an impossible angle. Morphine would help his pain, but if he had a head injury…

She examined him carefully but swiftly—breathing fine, heart rate steady, no blood that she could see and no outward sign of a head injury. His pupils responded to the light of a torch she'd borrowed from the attendant who hovered by her side.

Morphine could affect later examinations if the man had a head injury, but he needed pain relief…

'You have splints? Morphine?'

He nodded and went off to get what was needed, and Kate moved on.

The next patient was barely conscious and the rasping noises he was making suggested damage to a lung.

Kate quickly searched the man's chest for a puncture wound of some kind, but found nothing, although the man's gasp when she pressed gently against his ribs suggested one or more could be broken. She tipped the man's head back and saw the slight deviation in the line of his trachea, tapped his chest on the opposite side of the deviation, and heard a hollow drum sound.

'Get Dr Fareed,' she said to the attendant, who'd returned with a package of splint material and morphine.

Back at the first man, she gave him morphine to ease his pain, hoping it wouldn't interfere with any examination he would have at the hospital, then straightened his leg and was in the process of splinting it when Fareed arrived.

She pointed to her second patient.

'I'm thinking tension pneumothorax, so we'll need to release the trapped air and put in a chest drain but I don't know how much you do on site. I think—'

But Fareed was already inserting a needle between the man's ribs, into the pleural space where air, escaping from a damaged lung, was slowly compressing not only his lung but his heart, as well.

"That will relieve him for the moment, and we'll do the drain when he gets to hospital. Could you do a note to send with him and get him away?'

Kate jotted down what had been done for the man, checked the oxygen mask the attendants had in place, and handed him over.

Moving on, squatting, checking, speaking quietly to each patient, assuring and reassuring, hoping they'd understand her tone if not her words.

Fareed must have found more critically injured people because the four ambulances in attendance had already gone screaming down the dangerous road. She watched him move among the others, as reassuring as she was, always ready to listen, holding one man's hand as he tried to sit, patting his shoulder, speaking gently all the time.

All doctors are kind, she told herself as she returned to her most worrisome patient—the man with the broken femur. But the generalisation was wrong. She knew many men and women who, although wonderful, proficient medical professionals, insisted on keeping a professional distance from their patients. Courtesy was always there, but kindness? That was more rare...

She claimed the first ambulance that returned for her man with the broken femur, taking in the clamminess of his skin—worried that he might be going into shock.

The ambulance attendants lifted him onto a stretcher and into the back of the vehicle, Kate following, worrying—

'The doctors at the hospital are excellent—they'll take good care of him.'

She spun around to see Fareed right behind her.

'I was going to claim that ambulance for one of mine but I think you were right to get that man out of here fast. The complications of a break in the femur can be life-threatening.'

Another ambulance returned, then the third and the fourth, and they were able to load the rest of the casualties into these, some sitting by the stretcher in the side seats in each one.

Red taillights flickered in the darkness then disappeared, and Kate was left with Fareed in the eerie moonlight on the mountain whose jagged peaks looked like dark dinosaur teeth against the star-spangled purple velvet of the night sky.

It was a place of peace and beauty, and suddenly she longed to see it in daylight, to see all of it—the desert, the mountains, the sea. And the pain she'd felt when she'd accepted Ibrahim's bargain lessened, was replaced by the first stirrings of excitement.

'Some wedding night!' Fareed said, and Kate laughed not only at his words but because they'd broken into her thoughts at that precise moment. Not that he or wedding nights were any part of those stirrings.

Were they?

To distract herself, she waved her hands towards the view beneath them, the sands of the desert stretching to a distant sea, visible only as a deeper darkness than the sky.

'Where's the city?' she asked, puzzled that the lights of the towering buildings she had glimpsed there would not be visible.

'It is to the right, but hidden by the lower reaches

of the mountains and the trees in the fertile plains that lie at the foot of them. The winds from that direction bring rain and even snow, which falls in the mountains and drains down to that area.'

'An oasis?'

He paused before he replied, and when he said, 'Of such great beauty you could not imagine it,' his voice was full of pride and wonder and something else, that, to Kate's sensitive ears, could well have been love.

And could a man who loved his country be all bad?

Not that she thought him bad—just judgmental.

And if she wasn't feeling very tired and just a little disoriented, she probably would have ignored it, for didn't most people love their country?

Fareed studied her in the light of the moon, a small woman, gazing out over the desert, drinking in the beauty of it, her lips slightly parted, the sprinkle of freckles on her pert nose barely visible.

'I am grateful for your help tonight,' he said, and wondered if she'd heard him for it took a moment or two for her to turn and face him.

'I am here to be a doctor for a year. If you could just think of me that way, it would make things easier for both of us. So we're married at the moment, but really that means nothing. Let's just get on with being colleagues.'

It made sense, yet the knowledge that she'd been bribed to come here—bribed to marry him—bit deeply into his pride and aroused such suspicion, of her as well as his uncle, he knew he couldn't let down his guard. This woman might act all innocent, but her deal was with his uncle and though he loved his uncle, he knew the man could have taught Machiavelli a few lessons in deviousness.

'Shouldn't we be getting back to the hospital? Won't the staff on duty need more help with that influx of patients?'

She was making sense again—of course they had to get down to the hospital. He could hardly dislike her for being sensible, although he could regret that she was being sensible right now, when he'd have liked to have lingered on the mountain and watch a slim, pale woman with white skin and red-gold hair take in the beauty of his country.

'Are you always sensible?' he demanded, as he drove them back down the precipitous road.

'Nearly always,' she said, in such a way he had to wonder when she hadn't been. She'd shown no sign of regret about coming here—why would she if she was being offered vast sums of money?—so it must have been something in her past.

A man?

What kind of man would appeal to her?

And why the *hell* did it matter to him?

Would it be so hard to act as she was acting, and not only treat her as a fellow professional but accept her as such?

But they'd reached the plains and he heard her gasp and turned to see her face light up with excitement and her lips part as she breathed the word, 'Camels!'

His groin stirred—again!

Perhaps it *was* because it was his wedding night—not that he'd been looking forward to going to bed with any strange woman, let alone deflowering a virgin, as his bride had suggested—but maybe the words *wedding night* had subconsciously stirred up his libido, which would explain why it was playing up right now.

She had twisted around in her seat to catch a last glimpse of the camel train they'd passed—a string of at least twenty stately beasts travelling in the cool of the night—so he was able to study her and keep some of his attention on the road.

He wondered if his uncle had chosen her because she was the antithesis of the women he usually dated—either blondes or brunettes, always tall and beautifully groomed. Women who knew the world and how relationship games were played—women he'd liked enough to enjoy their time together but had never had regrets about when they or he moved on.

He'd put it down to the disaster that had been his parents' marriage, this inability he had to enter into even a semipermanent relationship with a woman, always finding an excuse to back away before things became too serious—before one of them was hurt…

Something about this woman told him she wouldn't have a clue.

Which was why he had to stop—right now—thinking of her as a woman at all and concentrate on her as nothing more than a colleague, in spite of the fact that she was, of course, his wife.

CHAPTER SIX

'IS THAT THE HOSPITAL? I can't believe it. I've never seen anything so fantastic in my life.'

The building resembled a long, low-slung tent, dark in colour, although it was a tent with the sides rolled up so light showed from within, through windows up to three stories high.

But it was the forecourt that stole Kate's breath away. It gave the impression of a giant Persian carpet, although it had to be made up of tiny tiles, not material. And set squarely in the middle of the carpet was a piece of artwork, something she couldn't name because it wasn't a statue but a representation of a campfire, warm and welcoming, flames flickering, although she knew they must be an optical illusion of some kind.

'It's done with lasers,' Fareed explained, as he drew into a parking area off the magic carpet. 'The carpet and the fire are symbols of welcome for the Bedouin people, from whom most of us are descended. The desert is too dangerous to turn away a stranger, so the carpet and the fire—and you'll see a coffee pot by it if you go closer—they say welcome.'

'And the shape of the hospital—it's a Bedouin tent?'

Fareed smiled in reply, and although Kate knew it was tiredness playing havoc with her emotions, she found herself smiling back.

As he held the door and helped her down from the high vehicle, Fareed tried to forget about the smile. He studied his colleague dispassionately. There was a smear of dirt on her cheek that he was tempted to wipe away—sliding his thumb across her skin. Her clothes were grubby from their hours on the mountain, and tiredness had smudged dark shadows under her eyes and drawn lines down her cheeks.

Yet she stepped briskly away from him and walked towards the building, still looking around, taking it all in, turning back to him to ask if the cluster of palms were date palms.

For some obscure reason her interest—no, her *obvious* interest and even more obvious delight—pleased him, even made her seem attractive to him.

Or maybe that was exhaustion, both emotional and physical…

'I need to wash and grab some scrubs before I see any patients,' she said, bringing him back to the reality that the night had not yet ended.

'I'll introduce you to someone who can fix you up,' he said, and hoped he sounded as matter-of-fact as she had.

But as he handed her over to one of the nurses on duty he felt a strange sensation that couldn't possibly have been loss.

Time to pull himself together—there was work to do and no way could he start feeling anything at all for this woman. She'd been right when she'd said all they had to do was work as colleagues—she was just another doctor.

But when she appeared with the too-big set of scrubs swamping her figure, the legs and arms rolled up so she could actually move around without falling over, he couldn't help but notice that the green of the garment made her eyes look greener, and the shower had brought some colour to her cheeks.

She held out her arms for his inspection then grinned at him.

'Like being an intern again, isn't it, working double shifts and getting that wonderful second wind halfway through the night.'

'Maybe I'd better have a shower and hope I get it, too,' he grouched, more disturbed by his reaction to the woman than his tiredness.

How could he possibly find her attractive? She just wasn't his type. And then there was the hair, which, while nothing like his mother's lustrous tresses, was definitely a reminder of childhood pain he had no wish to remember.

Kate watched him go and felt a little lost, but that was only because she was among strangers in a facility she didn't know. She wandered through the large admissions area. There were a few men seated as if waiting for treatment, or perhaps waiting for a loved one who was being treated, and some of the less injured patients from the bus were also sitting around.

Finding the desk where the paperwork would be done—and what hospital didn't have one?—she introduced herself and was steered towards treatment room six, where a pregnant woman lay on an examination couch, a female nurse taking her blood pressure through the cloth that covered her arm.

Cloth covered all her body, in fact, from the top of her head to the tip of her toes—a long robe, slippers, a hijab over her head and hair, and a mask of some kind that allowed only her eyes to shine through.

Anxious eyes.

Hiding her surprise that the bus-crash victims weren't getting priority, Kate stared at the woman, wondering where to begin. She needed to listen to the woman's chest and heartbeats and didn't want to do it through what looked like layers of material.

'How much do you know?' she asked the nurse.

The young nurse gestured to a computer screen—a very modern hospital—where a note explained the patient was twenty-eight weeks pregnant and had been experiencing some bleeding. Her blood pressure was slightly low but there was no other indication of trouble.

'Is there an obstetrician on call to see patients like this?' Kate asked, and the nurse nodded.

'I have called him, he is on his way.'

So what am I supposed to do? Kate wondered.

Examine the woman, presumably.

She began with the obvious, asking her patient if she spoke English.

'No, she doesn't, but her husband does. We could ask him to come in but Dr Fareed prefers the women to handle their own consultations. I can translate.'

Kate glanced at the earnest young nurse and didn't doubt that she could, but would this woman speak even to her?

'Could you tell her I'm going to listen to her heart and then to the baby's heartbeat. I'll be sliding the stethoscope inside her clothes to put it on her skin.'

The woman struggled into a sitting position.

'Better and better,' Kate said. 'I can check her lungs, as well.'

But as she approached the woman began to scream and within a minute there was a large, robed man in the room with them.

The nurse spoke harshly to him—words Kate couldn't understand—but she put her hand on the nurse's arm and steered her away, facing the man herself.

'Do you speak English?' she asked.

'A little,' he said. His guttural tones did nothing to ease Kate's concern but husbands accompanied their wives on prenatal visits in most places, so why not here?

'I'd be happy to have your help,' she said to the man, and held out her hand. 'I'm Dr Kate.'

The man ignored her hand and moved to stand protectively beside his wife.

It took time, but finally Kate was able to establish, by using her stethoscope on the square inches of flesh the man revealed through partings in his wife's clothes, that the woman was healthy and the baby's heartbeat was strong. She entered the information into the computer and was wondering how to tackle the next hurdle—the blood loss—when the obstetrician arrived.

Introducing himself as Akbar, he wasted little time in ordering the husband to take a seat over by the wall—still in the examination room but out of the way.

He then won Kate over completely by washing his hands, donning gloves then lifting the woman's skirts and drawing them up over her abdomen. The nurse, obviously used to his ways, draped a small sheet modestly over the woman's belly.

'You have to be firm with them,' he said to Kate. 'We understand he's anxious about his wife, as he should be—it's a first baby—but you can't let the men bully you. We need women doctors but they must be strong women doctors.'

He finished his examination and was stripping off his gloves.

'You strong?' he asked Kate.

'I think so,' she said.

The man nodded at her and favoured her with a charming smile.

'Good,' he said. 'I'll see you around. In the meantime, I want this woman admitted to the maternity ward at the hospital. That way I can keep her in bed for a week and see if the bleeding settles down. Send her home and she'll be back shopping and cooking and cleaning and probably grooming her husband's camels, and what she needs is rest.'

Kate returned his smile.

'Are you going to tell him or am I?'

Akbar put his hand on her shoulder.

'This one time I'll do it, but the referrals usually come from this place so it will be up to you in future.'

The hand on her shoulder was such a casual gesture Kate thought nothing of it until Fareed entered the already crowded room.

He spoke to Akbar and Kate wondered if the

harshness in his voice was because of the language or something else.

Not that she had to wonder for long. Leaving the nurse to make the transfer arrangements, she went to the desk, seeking more work.

'That man is a lech, steer clear of him.'

Fareed was right behind her, and although she understood exactly what he meant, she decided to ignore him. They were both tired and telling Fareed she was quite capable of looking after herself—*and* recognising a lech when she met one—would be pointless right now and probably provoke an argument.

Though why he should care did bother her a little. Surely it wasn't a possession thing—*you're my wife, therefore...*

She shook the thought away and found the next patient to whom she'd been assigned. This *was* one of the bus victims, but he needed nothing more than a few stitches in a gash in his arm, a dressing on it and a general health check to make sure they hadn't missed anything major.

Two patients later, as Kate's second wind had faded completely and she was wondering if there was such a thing as a third wind, Fareed appeared.

'The staff on the new shift are arriving—they'll double up for a while to clear the backlog of patients so we can go home.'

Home! The word caught unexpectedly at Kate's heart and she had to blink suddenly.

'Home where?' she demanded, probably sounding more aggressive than she'd intended because of her sudden fatigue.

'We'll go back to the palace.' Fareed was watching her closely. Had he seen the weakness? 'There are three bedrooms in that suite, there's no reason why we shouldn't use them, especially as our clothes are there.'

'His, hers and theirs?' Kate asked, trying desperately to make light of the situation, although returning to that ornate bedroom in the palace filled her with misgiving.

But Fareed was not amused.

'Exactly,' he said. 'There's no need for us to hide away in hospital accommodation when we can be more comfortable there. And you'll have the pool to swim in and the courtyard should you wish to be outside.'

He had taken her arm and was walking her towards the exit as he spoke. She wanted to pull away. He was too close—deliberately close—as if he wanted that closeness so his body could talk to hers.

Or was it nothing more than politeness on his part and the only body doing any talking was hers? Talking to *her*, telling her it was enjoying the closeness.

Surely not!

They reached the vehicle and something in the way he regarded her seemed to suggest it *hadn't* only been her body.

Desperate to get all thoughts of the man and the way her body was reacting to him out of her head, she went for lightness.

'And will we have to ruffle up the big marriage bed every morning to make it look as if we've slept in it?'

The look he was giving her intensified, and a small smile played around his lips.

'I didn't say *I* wouldn't use the bed,' he murmured, and a shiver of pure excitement ran down Kate's spine.

More likely it was fear, her head muttered as she hauled herself up into the passenger seat in an attempt to escape both the man and the feelings he was generating in her body.

And she *was* tired—emotions were always more raw when one was tired.

But was attraction stronger? Particularly unwanted attraction?

Why would it be?

Of course, it had to be the tiredness—why else would she be feeling it?

Fareed drove home with a feeling of satisfaction, knowing he'd rattled his new wife's composure.

He'd discovered it was fun to tease her just a little—to watch her react then hide her reaction with smart talk.

Though the word *home* had hit her hard. Just what could Ibrahim possibly have promised her to make her come so far from a place she obviously loved?

And, to his surprise, Fareed found himself wondering how he could make things easier for her—only as far as her being homesick was concerned. She was still a conniving, money-hungry woman who, instead of selling her soul to the devil, had sold it to Ibrahim. But he didn't like the people around him being unhappy.

That was probably why it had taken him so long to realise his mother didn't love him. He had been a fool to think that love had been the reason she'd sent for him as soon as she'd arrived on one of her rare visits to the palace. He had thought spending time with him had made her happy, never dreaming that she'd endured his presence so they could have a photo taken together in order to wring more money out of his father.

As he turned onto the road leading to the palace, he realised the sun had yet to rise. Given all that had happened, the previous sunrise might have been a week ago, but, no, he could see the colour in the eastern sky and knew the great red orb would soon be rising over the desert sands—a sight he loved so passionately he *had* to see it now.

And for some reason he felt an insistent desire to show it to Kate.

She was resting her head against the window and had her eyes closed as he turned off the palace road and onto a rough track that would lead to the top of the closest dune. The vehicle jolted as it left the tarmac, and Kate straightened in her seat.

'Oh, we're in the desert. It's hard to realise it's

right there, so close to the city, although I suppose the city was built on it.'

She turned to look at him.

'Where are we going?'

'To see the sunrise,' he said, and enjoyed the look of surprise on her face.

'Just a little farther and we turn towards the east. See?'

He spun the car and then looked out towards the painted sky, rich with pink and purple, orange streaked, the desert sand beneath the horizon reflecting back the vivid colours.

'Can I get out? Walk in the sand to watch it?'

'It's what I always do,' he told her, surprised by the pleasure he felt at her request, and as he watched her peel off her sneakers he felt a sense of pride in this woman who was his wife.

'I wanted to feel the sand between my toes,' she explained when he joined her on the very top of the dune, so they could see the city below them to the right, and in front of them the first red glow of the sun rising majestically above the horizon.

'Oh, Fareed, that is so beautiful!'

The whispered words, full of genuine wonder, shifted something in his chest, and although he knew touching her was fraught with danger, he slid an arm around her shoulders and held her close until the sun completed its wondrous act and the colours faded to gentler tones, reflecting *their* colour on his companion's fair skin.

Kissing her had definitely not been on the agenda—any agenda, not ever—but the stirring inside him must have provoked a momentary madness, for he bent and touched his lips to hers—a breath of a touch, no more. But the moment skin met skin, a fiery longing seized him and he wanted nothing more than to devour those pale lips and slide his tongue along the pearly teeth, and take her, right here and now, as his bride.

He'd touched his lips to hers, and suddenly she was all aquiver. Kate edged away from him because that touch, though she knew it was a kind of 'the end' to the bit of magic they'd shared with the sunrise, had set her nerves jangling through her body and had stirred up all the fight-or-flight reactions that came from the area of her brain that warned of danger.

Danger with a capital D.

She hoped Fareed hadn't noticed her response, hadn't felt it in her body or tasted in on her lips.

Maybe he had, for he was studying her, the mask that hid all his thoughts back in place.

Had she upset him?

She hadn't meant to, so she rushed into speech, hoping to cover the awkward moment.

'That was the most beautiful experience,' she told him, as she edged back towards the open passenger-side door then realised she'd timed it badly. 'The sunrise, I mean,' she added, desperate to recover lost ground. 'Thank you so much for sharing it with me.'

She scrambled into the car then discovered, once he was in, that they were far too close to each other.

'I'm obviously not used to doing all-night duty,' she muttered. 'Please tell me we're not on again until tomorrow—or *I'm* not on again until tomorrow?'

He glanced her way then turned his attention back to the road.

'You don't *have* to work, you know.'

'I came here to work,' she told him. 'For me, that was the main reason. The marriage thing was just Ibrahim's bargain. But surely he told the truth when he said you need doctors and that I'd be usefully employed?'

Another glance, this one a little grim but that was probably because she'd used the M word.

'We do need doctors with ER experience, I won't

deny that. Ibrahim and I have different views on the sex of the doctors. He would like a lot more women working here so women could always see a woman doctor.'

'And you don't agree?'

He sighed.

'It's complicated. It's not the women doctors. I have nothing but respect for them and, in fact, find many of them far more suited to ER work than men, who don't see it as a career path but—' He stopped abruptly, adding more quietly, 'We'll talk about it some other time. Let's get back to the palace. Shall I order you some breakfast so you can eat before you sleep?'

Hmm, Kate thought. *So you don't really want to talk about this disagreement. I must remember to bring it up again, if only because it just might give me some insight into how you think.*

But, 'Breakfast would be lovely,' was all she said for now. 'Can we eat out in the courtyard again?'

Foot in mouth again with that 'we' but she wasn't going to try to take it back. Surely eating breakfast together wasn't going to compromise either of them.

CHAPTER SEVEN

SHE ATE ALONE, a delicious meal of fruit and pastries and yoghurt topped with honey. Ate too much but her tired body needed fuel.

Back inside the wedding room, she found the sumptuous bed turned down, ready for an occupant.

Or two?

No, hadn't Fareed said he'd sleep in it?

In which case she'd have to find another way in and out of the courtyard, because it was beginning to feel like a special sanctuary to her.

Fareed appeared as she was mulling over this.

'You might as well use the bed,' he said. 'The wife's bedroom in this suite is through the dressing room and has no direct access to the courtyard.'

Only to the husband's bedroom? Kate wondered. And was it access for her or for him?

Bur Fareed had made his suggestion and departed and she didn't really want to know the answers to her questions anyway. It was only tiredness playing with her mind.

She pulled off her clothes, had a quick shower. Tomorrow she'd try some of the lotions and potions. She pulled on a her favourite pyjamas—a present from Billy and soft from many washings, the pattern of tiny frogs almost completely washed away—and climbed into the enormous bed.

It was like lying on a cloud, so softly did it wrap around her. She snuggled deeper and—

Woke to darkness, and a small night-light burning somewhere over by the window, so she could take stock of where she was. Still half-asleep, she brought to mind the events of the past twenty-four—or maybe thirty-six—hours.

Slowly she let the images roll through her head—the wedding gaiety, her as a parcel, Fareed's disgust, but even as he'd felt it, him being kind in his own way. The accident and getting back to work—always a good thing—then the sunrise—

She shut down the film show, not wanting to go further, but, thinking of the sunrise, she realised she must have slept through a whole day for it to be dark again.

Reaching for the bedside light, she must have

touched a sensor on the base for it sprang to life, casting a soft glow across her side of the bed.

Her side of the bed?

Did Fareed have a side he preferred?

Silly thought when she'd never have the opportunity to find out, and wasn't even thinking about it a waste of time?

She eased herself out of the cloud and headed for the dressing room. Obviously his side of the bed would be the other side because his dressing room was that side!

She shook her head, hoping to regain the sanity she'd need to get through the day—or night, as it happened to be.

But once in the dressing room, the dilemma of actually dressing seized her. What was she supposed to be doing next? Where was she supposed to be now she was awake?

Who was she supposed to be?

The soft knock on a side door of the room was so welcome she called, 'Come in,' before considering who it might be.

Or realising the room beyond that door would be Fareed's dressing room.

He was wearing dark slacks and a lighter polo

top that must have been silk the way it clung so lovingly to his chest and shoulders, and her heart scrunched a little in her chest in the realisation that all of this was just pretend.

'I saw the light and thought you might be feeling a little lost,' he said, the words kind enough, though his attention seemed to be centred on her night attire.

'Wedding-night finery?' he added, the slight smile she'd seen before just a suggestion on his lips.

'Comfort after a long day,' Kate said, and hated sounding so defensive. 'But what comes next? Do we hide away in here, venturing out only to go to work, or is there stuff we should be doing, people we should see?'

She flung out her arms. 'I haven't a clue what I'm doing in this place!'

'Earning whatever Ibrahim is paying you, I imagine,' Fareed replied, then immediately regretted the bitter remark. But he'd walked in and seen her in her ridiculous pyjamas, her hair escaping from the plait so bits of it stood up everywhere. She'd looked like a sleepy child but, unfortunately, not enough like a child for his body not to react to her presence.

His reaction and the fact that he'd hit out at her,

if only verbally, annoyed him to the extent he'd have liked to turn on his heel and walk away, but that first image of the child—a lost child—held him back.

'If you press a blue button either by your bed, in your bathroom off the dressing room or on a desk in the little day room beyond the bedroom, someone will come. You can order food, clothes, a car—whatever you might want.'

Now he could turn and walk away, although when he'd first come in it had been to—

'What if you get dressed and I'll take you to dinner?' he heard himself say, and cursed inwardly.

It *was* what he had intended saying earlier, as a way of thanking her for her help, but then the mention of his uncle and the unanswered questions about this relationship had reminded him he didn't want to get close to this woman, not even vaguely close.

So why had he asked her to dinner?

And, given how he'd just insulted her, would she come?

She was peering intently at him, frowning slightly as if not entirely sure who he was. And why wouldn't she be puzzled? He'd come in as a friend then had sniped almost immediately. But there was something more in her regard.

'No glasses?' he said. 'Can you see well enough to find them?'

The words broke whatever spell had enveloped her.

'They'll be by the bed, they always are,' she said, 'but I was wondering why you're asking me to dinner. You don't have to, you know. I'm happy just to work out my year at the hospital. I don't expect a social life.'

There was a trace of something just behind the words—regret? hurt?—but he didn't know her well enough to guess.

Would probably never know her well enough...

'One dinner is hardly a social life,' he muttered, somehow disturbed by the fact he *wouldn't* ever know her well enough.

This situation was ridiculous. She was just a woman, nice enough looking but not in the class of women he usually dated; what's more, she'd been bribed into marrying him by his uncle.

Which made her a conniving woman!

But as she seemed willing to work at the hospital and, thrown into the bus accident, had been more than competent, perhaps they could forget the marriage thing and get on with their lives.

Individual lives…

'Well, we *do* have to eat!' he added, determined now to get her to agree. Since when had a woman turned down one of *his* invitations?

She smiled suddenly, the expression lighting up her whole face so the pale skin seemed to glow from within.

'Okay!' she said. 'Give me ten minutes to pull on some clothes and— Oh!'

'Oh?'

'That's where I was when you came in. I've got clothes I brought from home, jeans and T-shirts and a couple of skirts and tops, then the women who swamped me with kindness before the wedding kept producing these long floaty trouser things with long tunics to go over them. Given you're a public figure and I'm supposed to be your wife, if we're going outside these rooms, should I wear one of those outfits?'

Could she really be as unworldly as she seemed? And have so little interest in clothes? The women he'd known in his life—all of them, from aunts and cousins to lovers and friends—were absorbed by clothes to the extent that asking his fashion advice would be as likely as them hesitating over a dinner invitation.

And, from the way she spoke, she'd only said yes because she thought maybe others would expect it of her.

Others like Ibrahim?

Though why should he, Fareed, care why she'd said yes? He'd only asked her out of kindness—pity really. After all, she *was* a stranger in a strange place.

'Wear trousers and a tunic,' he said. 'I'll meet you in the big bedroom in half an hour.'

'Okay,' she agreed. 'Only don't expect the fine clothes to suddenly turn me into a ravishing beauty, like in the stories where the secretary takes off her glasses and shakes out her hair and she's beautiful. With me, if I shake out my hair it's all tangles and if I take off my glasses I'm practically blind, so what you see is what you get, I'm afraid.'

She turned away before he'd made sense of the words—off to get her glasses, no doubt.

Had she been apologising for her looks?

He didn't think so—just telling it like it was. He remembered her on the mountain the night before. She hadn't hesitated about going with him, and once there she'd got straight to work and had worked through what had been left of the night without a murmur of complaint.

Remembered her, too, at sunrise, her face lit by her delight in the magical time that was so special to him, taking off her shoes to feel the sand between her toes...

Without doubt she was the strangest—no, that wasn't the word—perhaps the most beguiling woman he'd ever met!

And while she might not be a ravishing beauty, the sight of her ten minutes later in local dress, a pair of deep blue trousers with a sea-green and blue tunic, splashed somehow with gold thread, did something peculiar to his heartbeat. She had gold sandals dangling from her hand, and had somehow bunched her hair on the top of her head so she looked taller—womanly! And although he was fairly sure there was a light coating of make-up on her pale skin, the little gold freckles still shone through.

Kate knew she'd brushed up well—no ravishing beauty but passable by most standards—not that Fareed had anything to say about her looks, simply nodding to acknowledge her and leading her out of the door she'd first entered as a parcel late the previous afternoon. Or was it two afternoons ago? She'd lost count, but right now all she had to do was follow Fareed through the corridors of the palace.

And keep up if she didn't want to get lost!

She lengthened her stride in an effort to catch up to him then wondered if there was a protocol she didn't know.

'Am I *supposed* to walk two paces behind you?' she asked.

He looked so startled she had to smile.

'Of course not,' he muttered at her. 'Why ever should you?'

'I just wondered. You were going so fast it was hard to keep up then I thought maybe that's how it should be.'

He stopped, turned to stare at her and shook his head.

'It has *never* been like that, understand! Not from a servility point of view. In times past when no one knew what danger lay ahead, a man would walk in front of his womenfolk to protect them, but now—'

He stopped, shook his head again, and added, 'Let's talk about it over dinner.'

Upon which he strode off once again, leaving Kate to hurry behind, puzzling over what she'd done to annoy him this time.

The question of why Ibrahim had chosen this particular suite of rooms for the newly married couple continued to eat away at Fareed. He recalled all those times when he had rushed here on hearing his mother was in residence, hoping for the smallest show of affection, even permission to swim in the pool she never used. But, no, the cold, unhappy woman would allow him to kiss her cheek then she'd wrap an arm around him for the photographer and he'd be sent on his way—never a hug, or a word of love, nothing but the emptiness in his chest when he left the suite yet again.

He recalled the horror of finding his father, too… But he didn't want to think of that now—too many raw emotions…

A redhead and this suite… Was Ibrahim playing some deep game? Could it be that he didn't really feel the affection for his nephew that Fareed had always felt he had? Was Ibrahim perhaps regretting that Fareed was heir to the throne? Would his uncle have wanted it to go to one of his own children?

No, he couldn't believe that, although the thought left a hollow in his chest.

He'd been fooled by his mother, fooled into thinking—again and again—that she might actually love him. Surely he couldn't have been fooled by his uncle—not all this time—surely not…

He must have been striding again for he heard the shuffle of hurrying feet behind him. This time when he stopped he took her arm, and once he'd touched her, all thoughts of Ibrahim vanished like a wisp of cloud, his mind filled with the woman by his side, the feel of her arm beneath her tunic, the faint scent of rosewater—reminiscent of weeks he'd spent camping in the deepest desert with Bedouin relations.

Most of the women in the court—and women he had courted from without it—smelled of designer perfume, not the fragrance that was as much part of his life as his skin and bones and tissues.

'So, tomorrow do we go to work? I must say I'm excited to see more of the hospital you've built—to see what facilities it has and to learn the procedures you use regarding referrals to specialists, and hospitalisation.'

'Really?' he asked, glancing down at her, finding it hard to believe that a woman here purely for the money Ibrahim would pay her should be bothered about such things.

'Of course,' she said, glaring at him. 'I've told you I was here to work. How else am I going to fill in a year?'

He wanted to tell her most of the women he knew filled their time quite easily. Visits to the big malls where European and American designers displayed their wares, trips to the big international hotels for tea and cakes. Then they had appointments for their hair, their nails, their waxing and polishing, massages and yoga and perhaps a little not-too-strenuous gym work.

But he had a feeling if he told her this she would stare blankly at him, or possibly disbelieve him completely.

And to give her her due, she'd insisted on going to the accident site and had then worked in the hospital while she'd been needed.

'You haven't answered me.'

He looked at her, her eyes still on his face, and

for the life of him he couldn't remember what she'd asked, the sudden stirring of attraction towards her blotting out all thoughts.

Totally confused, he dropped a kiss on her lips— soft and pink and slightly open so he could see the pearl-like teeth.

'We'll talk about it later,' he said, and hoped he'd be able to go back through his thoughts to rescue the conversation.

She studied him a moment longer.

'That kiss was nothing but a diversionary tactic and don't think I don't know it,' she said. 'But if we're going to eat tonight, we should get going.'

Which they should, but his feet were stuck to the ground, and his body was demanding another kiss, a proper kiss, not a diversionary one, as she'd correctly said.

'Now?' she suggested.

He pulled himself together, took her arm again, and led her onwards, along the corridor that would eventually open near the old stables where the cars were kept.

But once outside it was she who slowed, for not all the stables were used for cars.

'Oh, look at that magnificent fellow,' she said,

pointing to where Fareed's stallion, Muhib, peered from his stall.

'Not tonight,' Fareed said firmly. 'Tomorrow I'll show you the horses.'

Though he had no idea why he'd made *that* offer!

A driver pulled up beside them in a low-slung, sporty coupe.

'I'll drive tonight, Ahmed,' Fareed told him, as he opened the passenger door and helped Kate inside. He pulled the seatbelt free and passed it to her, his hand accidentally brushing against her breast, and again, for all this was an arranged marriage that held nothing but questions for him, he felt the tightening of attraction.

Think of his disdainful face, Kate told herself. *The way he surveyed our property, and us, really, as if we were beneath him. And his jibes about Ibrahim's money. Just because he's taking you to dinner, and dropping careless kisses here and there, it doesn't mean a thing. Don't think of that sunrise; don't think of that kiss...*

But the casual kiss then the brush of his hand across her breast had set her heart racing. Apparently you didn't have to like someone to be attracted to him.

The thought was so bizarre, she pondered it as they drove to wherever he was taking her. She supposed attraction could work like that. After all, it was put into people to ensure they propagated and the human race lived on. Dogs didn't have to be in love to have sex, or horses, or—

'Do you enjoy seafood?'

She'd been about to add fish to her list of species, so his question made her smile.

'Very much so.'

'Good,' he said, as he approached a roundabout. Turning off it to the right, he drove a short distance onto an esplanade that ran along a sandy beach, the dark waters of the sea lit by silvery foam and, here and there, by the lights along the road.

He pulled up into a parking lot opposite a dilap- idated-looking shack, stopped the car, got out and came around to help her alight. She was already halfway out by the time he reached her, hurrying so there'd be no need for him to touch her again.

'It doesn't look all that great, but the seafood it sells will have been caught only hours earlier and you will get no finer food in Amberach.'

'Yet it looks quiet, almost deserted,' she said, as

they crossed the road and walked up a rickety jetty to where the shack perched above the water.

'Most locals and the expatriates prefer the fancy restaurants in the big hotels. This place doesn't have the ambiance they like.'

'But it's beautiful,' Kate whispered, as a young man bowed low to Fareed and led them to an outer veranda, where they sat above the sea and looked out at the moonlight playing on the water.

Was she genuine or was she simply doing what she felt she'd been paid to do?

Fareed wished he knew, although for now he was happy to give her the benefit of the doubt, because this was a special place and the faint flush on her face and the shine in her unpainted eyes suggested her words were genuine.

'May I order for you or would you prefer to choose dishes for yourself?' he asked, to get his mind back on the meal.

'Go ahead and order for me,' she said. 'There's no seafood I don't like.'

He ordered a lobster thermidor for her main course and for an appetiser a platter of tiny prawns, baby octopus, fish pieces, oysters and mussels, something they could share, picking at it as they talked.

If they talked!

He need not have worried. As they waited for the first part of the meal to arrive, she sipped at her water then asked, 'So, is tomorrow a workday?'

Fareed felt a twinge of disappointment. Here they were in one of the most romantic places in his land and she wanted to talk about work.

Of course she wanted to talk about work. What else would she want to talk about—the sham of a marriage she'd got herself into?

So he told her, yes, if she wished, she could work the next day.

'I'll get the staffing officer to draw up a roster for you,' he said, adding to himself, *leaving me off it as much as possible.*

'I think Ibrahim has already allocated you a driver. If you let him know the roster he will always be waiting for you.'

To his surprise, Kate smiled—and once again his body yelled attraction.

'Then I should probably ask for some extra bread to take back with me so I can leave a trail of breadcrumbs from the stables back to the suite. How else will I find my way there in the morning?'

He found himself smiling back. And ignoring his own warning to never work the same roster as her.

'I will take you there in the morning, show you around and introduce you properly. We will leave at eight, if that suits you.'

'That would be great, but please don't feel you have to look after me all the time. Once I've found my way around enough to get to the car and back to where I'm sleeping, I'll be fine.'

'You don't want to mix with the other women? You must have met some of them since you've been here. Your life shouldn't be all work.'

She studied him for a moment then sighed before explaining, 'I have met many of them and they have been wonderfully kind and supportive, but they are women with curiosity and I would be uncomfortable with them because of the pretence. I would rather work and sleep, swim in the pool, maybe do a little sightseeing, but I don't want to be answering questions about you, or my life with you. I don't want to deceive them. It was bad enough deceiving you on the drive from the airport but I had promised Ibrahim I'd say nothing.'

Fareed shook his head. In his experience women revelled in a little deception and intrigue and would have thought nothing of making up stories about their marriage, their husband and even his prowess—or otherwise—in the bedroom. Hadn't whispers of such things come back to him from women he had once thought loved him?

She was definitely different, this woman.

The food arrived and they began to eat, using their fingers to pick up the delicate morsels, using flat bread to savour the juices. Fingers brushed from time to time, but the conversation focused on the food, with Kate letting out little moans of delight with each new mouthful.

'This is so delicious,' she said. 'I've eaten this kind of food before but the spices and the way it's been cooked make it more delicious than anything I've ever had. The only trouble is, if I keep eating I won't be able to eat my lobster.'

'We can take our time,' Fareed said quietly, and Kate glanced up at him, trying to read behind the mask that was his face.

He was an enigma, this man. Definitely kind, caring even, yet he hid every emotion from view. Even when he'd kissed her in the corridor, shocking her into silence for a while, nothing had shown on his face.

Though he *had* smiled earlier, she reminded herself, then had to wonder if it had actually been a smile or a simple movement of his lips that had looked like a smile, but without any emotion behind it.

CHAPTER EIGHT

SHE DID FINISH her lobster, although by the end of the meal she knew she'd overdone it.

'I think I should walk back to the palace after that,' she told him, as she pushed away from the table.

Again what might have been a smile.

'That would be a bit drastic, but we could take a stroll along the beach.'

By the sea?

In the moonlight?

With this man to whom she already felt a fine, fragile thread of attraction?

I don't think so.

'That sounds lovely.'

She knew the words were hers, knew she'd said them, because even if she hadn't recognised her own voice she could feel the tension they had caused in her body.

They left their sandals and shoes on the path

along the foreshore, and walked down onto the sand, smooth and cool underfoot, sliding between Kate's toes.

'Is it the same sand as in the desert?' she asked, and he bent to lift a handful, letting it trickle into her out-held hand.

'The very same but the beach sand becomes bleached by the water while the desert sand retains the redness of the mountains from which it is born.'

She closed her fingers on it, feeling the warmth of it in her palm. Amberach sand—the world was a truly wonderful place and somehow she'd found herself in a particularly magical corner of it. Surely it was all right to enjoy it...

They had walked a little, paused, and walked again, but now Fareed asked what she was thinking and she tried to explain.

'I know I have been the means of putting you in a very awkward position, but I cannot regret coming here. It is so different, so special somehow, I wouldn't have missed it for anything.'

'Yet you have seen so little of it.'

'I'll see more, but look ahead—at the ridge of rock tumbling down into the sea, and the moon shining on the desert closer to where we are—these are beauties I had never imagined, and although it probably sounds daft to you, it touches my soul.'

'Not so daft,' he said quietly, then he bent his head and kissed her lips, very slowly and barely touching at first, although soon his mouth firmed on hers, his arms enclosed her, and she found herself responding, her lips parting at his insistence, and from her own desire.

A month at least, it lasted, that kiss.

It stole her breath, and teased her into thinking things she shouldn't think—things like marriage and marriage beds and—

Now his hands were moving on her skin—well, not skin but on the fine-woven silk of her tunic. He was learning her by feel, all the time keeping her pressed against him so she could feel his reaction to the kiss was as strong, and probably as startling, as her own.

'It is unseemly for a prince to be behaving like this in public.'

The husky whisper sent a shot of pure lust downwards through her body and she clung a little tighter.

Slowly he eased her off, took her hand, and began

to walk back to where they'd left the car—*and* their footwear.

No words spoken—no laughing off the kiss—it was as if they were held in a bubble that existed beyond this world. A bubble of both time and place that could burst any minute with one false step or one unconsidered word...

He had to think! Had to stop kissing this stranger—who was his wife—and try to work out exactly what was going on in Ibrahim's mind. Heaven forbid he take her to bed—which he desperately wanted to do—and she became pregnant...

Was that Ibrahim's plan?

No! There was no way on this earth or the next Ibrahim could possibly have realised that some peculiar chemistry would attract the two of them to each other. Ibrahim knew the type of women he dated—the kind of women to whom he was attracted.

And surely Ibrahim knew him well enough to know a red-haired woman was more likely to repel him than attract him.

He glanced towards the woman at the centre of this puzzle—big mistake, as she was looking out the window but smiling at the same time—a soft, beguiling kind of smile that made him want to stop the car and kiss her all over again.

Then rip her clothes off and—

Some echo of the groan he'd thought he'd concealed deep inside his body must have escaped for she turned to look at him, concern on her face.

'Are you okay?' she asked, spreading soft fingers on his arm.

'As can be!' he answered roughly, then regretted it, but it was better to be back at odds with her than the attraction thing.

Could it be genetic, this attraction to a red-haired woman? His father had been besotted, and then destroyed…

Was Ibrahim testing him, marrying him to Kate? Testing his strength of character—his ability to be heir to the Sultanate?

Growing up in the palace, he'd heard enough gossip about his parents to know his mother had expected to become a queen immediately she'd married, not realising the old sultan, Fareed's grandfather, had still been alive.

And so she'd left—left her little son and her husband—returning only when she'd wanted money, tormenting her husband until—

He pulled into the castle grounds, and drove more slowly towards the converted stables, reluctant now to leave this woman, yet...

She'd lost him.

Somewhere between the kiss and the car, she thought. Not that she'd wanted more—

Liar!

Attraction was a peculiar thing. Here she'd been, thinking a marriage of convenience would be safe from attraction—from the longings, and stirrings, and demanding needs of desire.

Especially after Mark, who, for all his declarations of undying love, had dropped her like a hot potato when she'd said she had to go home. No sympathy, no hint of understanding, just, 'Well, if you go don't expect me to wait.'

So much for love!

Not that this was love—it was far too urgent, too primal to be covered by that gentle word...

Now her husband, the man she didn't know yet had kissed with passion, led her back to the suite, suggested she continue to use the big bed, and departed, leaving behind an emptiness Kate couldn't understand.

* * *

Waking in the morning, determined not to brood on Fareed's peculiar behaviour the previous evening, Kate dressed, ate her breakfast, then asked the maid to take her to where she'd meet her driver.

Fareed wasn't anywhere in sight when she reached the hospital, but a nurse she'd met the day of the accident showed her around. They'd barely covered the important things when three young women, covered in the all-concealing black cloaks called *abayas*, their hair hidden by scarves, appeared in the waiting room and greeted Kate with cries of delight.

'Oh, thank goodness you are here. We did hope we'd get a woman doctor but getting you is even better. You have an oath thing, don't you, doctors? You can't talk about what we tell you?'

Mai, Suley and Farida crowded around her and while assuring them all of confidentiality she ushered them into an examination cubicle and drew the curtains to close it off.

'I didn't recognise you at first in your cloaks. So, what is wrong?'

The young women—girls, really—looked puzzled, then Farida caught on.

'You mean the *abayas*? We always wear them when we go somewhere public like the mall but this time we wore them so we could come here without anyone recognising us as part of the royal family and fussing over us.'

'I see,' Kate said, as they settled themselves, Mai and Suley on the examination couch and Farida on the only chair.

Kate propped herself on the equipment cabinet and studied them. There was something wrong—not health-wise, she suspected—but...

She didn't have a clue. It wasn't drugs or alcohol, they were all too healthy looking.

'So?' she asked, and waited, until, slowly and with obvious reluctance, Mai pulled back one sleeve of her black, all-enveloping gown.

Kate's heart missed a beat at the sight of the bandaged wrist, although there didn't appear to be blood staining the bandage so maybe the damage had been minimal.

'Want to tell me about it?' she said, as she gently unwrapped the bandage.

As usual it was Farida who took over the explanations.

'We were—we thought—we...'

But the usually confident Farida faltered and now Suley, her arm around Mai, hung her head and whispered the words Kate needed to hear.

'We had this silly idea, back when we were children. We decided that we didn't want to be married off to just anyone. We wanted to be free to choose our own husbands. We took a vow and pricked our fingers and mixed our blood, that we would all stand together and…'

Suley stopped, obviously unable to go on, but Kate could guess at what the young women had decided.

She had laid bare the cuts on Mai's arm, not deep but reddened at the edges. She could use a couple of stitches in one of them but guessed that was the last thing Mai would want.

A nurse appeared at the end of the curtained room but Kate stepped in front of her young friend and sent the nurse away.

Finding antiseptic and butterfly sutures, she bathed the wounds and put the strips of tape across the cuts to hold them together. She was nearly done when Suley spoke again.

'This was my fault. My father told me last night that he'd chosen my husband, and I phoned the others to meet me at the mall. We went into one of the restrooms and I had a razor blade but I was too scared to cut myself, so Mai said she'd show me how, then she saw the blood and fainted and we didn't know what to do, then Farida remembered you might be working here and could help us.'

'My father will kill me if he finds out I did this,' Mai whispered, 'and poor Suley, what can we do to help her?'

Kate was fitting a clear adhesive dressing over the wound but her mind was churning with the scraps of information she'd been given.

'There,' she said, as she finished. 'Now, tell me the plan you had back when you swore the oath and mingled your blood.'

Farida must have recovered her confidence for it was she who spoke.

'We were all going to kill ourselves,' she announced, and Kate had to hide a smile at the melodrama of youth, although by now they should have had more sense.

'I imagine you were about ten years old and the drama of it was so exciting you didn't think past the actual act. Killing yourself is so very final, you know. You end up dead before you've had time to think of all the wonderful things in life you're going to miss out on—university, careers, love, children and just having fun. There's no coming back from dead—or very rarely.'

'But it was to be a protest to our families,' Mai told her. 'How else could we make them realise that arranged marriages are so out of date—that we should be allowed to choose our own partners.'

Kate took a deep breath.

'I really do not know enough about your customs to talk about such things, but surely—'

The curtain opened again and this time it was Fareed who stalked through.

'I will see these girls, Dr Andrews,' he said crisply.

'I don't think so,' Kate replied, feeling Mai hurriedly hiding her wrist behind her. 'They actually wanted to see a woman doctor.'

'That's as may be,' Fareed muttered, 'but they are related to me, I know their parents and I just heard you say something about not understanding our customs.'

'That doesn't lessen my effectiveness as a doctor,' Kate snapped, 'so now I'd like you to leave so I can continue my consultation.'

He stood there, glaring at her, and for a moment she thought she might have won the argument, then he drew in a deep breath and began again.

'The women in this country, the young ones in particular, want gender equality. It is my opinion that if they are so eager for it, they should accept it in all aspects of their lives. They should be just as willing to see a male doctor as a female one.'

Kate straightened her spine and fought back.

'For some things, yes, and I'm sure they would be. But there are some things, I, as a woman, would prefer to discuss with a woman doctor, just as you would probably prefer to discuss something like— oh, impotence—with a male doctor.'

She heard the collective gasp from the young women behind her, and saw colour leach from Fareed's face as anger fired his eyes and stiffened his body.

'I will talk to you later,' he said, each word delivered like a death threat.

And with a final slit-eyed glare he left the cubicle.

'Is he really impotent?' Suley whispered, and with a groan Kate dropped her head into her hands, shook her head, and wondered what on earth she had done.

Of all the things to have said, and in front of witnesses, but he'd made her so angry, so furious, the words had just come tumbling out.

'No, he's not, it was nothing more than an example of what a man might not wish to discuss with a woman doctor.'

She looked sternly at the three, adding, 'And if any one of you mention this outside this cubicle I will tell everyone about your silliness. Now, let's get back to it.'

They nodded in unison, but were still watching her, wide-eyed with awe.

'Firstly, tell me this, do you all love your parents?'

Three more nods.

'Can you talk to them both, or to one or other of them, about most things?'

'I can talk to my mother about absolutely anything,' Suley said, 'and Farida's parents are fantastic, they are more like an older sister and brother than parents—we all talk to them about sex and boys and stuff.'

'And you, Mai?' Kate asked gently.

'Usually I can,' she said, 'to both my parents, although they are quite strict. All our parents are strict as far as our behaviour goes, like we're not allowed to go out with boys alone, or go to night-clubs.'

'Could you tell them what has happened?'

Suley shook her head.

'My father would be very angry. He would say I was stupid and how could a stupid girl like me go away to college?'

'Farida, could you explain this to your parents?'

Farida was quiet for a while then asked, 'But why would I need to?'

'I'm just worried one or other of your sets of parents will hear about this visit to the hospital from Fareed and you will be asked to explain. Although there is confidentiality between you and me, I must fill out some kind of information about your visit and he, as head of the hospital, can easily access it. If the three of you would be happy to explain it all to someone like Farida's parents, they could settle the other parents down before it blows up into something far bigger than it was.'

The three spoke among themselves, quickly in their own language, finally facing Kate again.

'Would you come with us to Farida's house? Would you explain?'

Kate looked at three pairs of beseeching brown eyes.

'I could,' she said, 'but not until my shift ends. Could you go back to the mall until four and I'll meet you there then?'

Apparently this presented no problem. Kate asked when Mai had last had a tetanus injection, checked the dressing on her wrist, suggested she buy some bangles at the mall to cover it, and sent them on their way.

Fareed must have been watching from somewhere because she'd no sooner left the cubicle than he appeared beside her.

'What happened with those girls?' he demanded.

'I sorted it,' Kate said, trying hard to ignore the signals his body was sending hers, as well as the anger that was simmering behind his eyes.

'But they are family, I must speak to their parents.'

'I'm doing that later,' Kate said, as airily as her tension would allow. 'They knew me, you know. They were part of the entourage that helped me prepare for the wedding and were with me at the henna party. I'm sure that's why they asked for me, rather than for you.'

She knew he wasn't appeased and she was probably adding fuel to the fire, but she couldn't resist adding, 'And there is such a thing as patient confidentiality, you know!'

He greeted this with a derisive snort and stormed away, leaving Kate shaken by the encounter and upset that she'd torn apart whatever tentative bonds they'd forged the previous night.

A little sadness seeped into her soul because, for all her bold talk of it being nothing more than sexual attraction, she was beginning to see that other emotions were mixed up in her feelings for Fareed.

She was without doubt *the* most infuriating woman he had ever met! Firstly, defying him when he'd demanded to take over her patients, then accusing him of impotence—him!

And in front to those silly young women!

It would be all over Amberach, and believed, given his own bride had said it.

He'd kill her!

Somewhere in the ancient laws of his tribal ancestors there had to be one that covered insolence towards the crown prince, and he was certain it would be punishable by death.

Unfortunately, death was so very permanent and every time he looked at the wretched woman he had a jolt of lust rush through his body—lust, he knew, that wouldn't be satisfied by just any woman right now.

Maybe he could imprison her in the suite—in the bedroom—tied to the bed...

His groin stirred painfully and he cursed again, unable to believe where his thoughts had strayed.

Fortunately he was called to another patient, a woman, while he was pleased to see a robed man objecting when he was led towards Kate and introduced to her as his doctor.

She glanced across the wide room and raised her eyebrows and he could almost hear her asking if gender equality shouldn't work both ways.

The man, he realised, was refusing to be seen by Kate, who treated him with respect and suggested he sit down and wait until a male doctor was available.

The man was voluble in his protests but just then an ambulance attendant brought in a young labourer with an obviously horrific wound to his arm and shoulder.

Kate hurried the pair into the cubicle, calling for

a nurse and a pathology runner to take blood to the lab.

Every instinct told him he should go to this case, but the woman he'd been walking to a cubicle was groaning now, and he realised she was definitely in labour.

All part of a day's work in the ER.

Kate sat the young man on the bed so recently vacated by her friends, and listened as the ambulance attendant gave his report. Her patient had already been given morphine for the pain and had fluid running into his good arm.

The man had fallen on a building site, probably about twenty feet, but he'd brought down a pile of bricks with him, and they had landed on his arm and shoulder.

Kate cleaned the wound as best she could, picking out bits of brick and grit.

'We'll take him through to X-Ray,' she told the nurse who'd appeared to help her.

The nurse called for an orderly, who wheeled the man through to the back of the main room, where every kind of machine was set up to provide the very best of patient information.

An X-ray was all Kate needed now, but she was

pleased to see an echocardiogram and what looked like a nuclear scanner.

The X-ray clearly showed a compound fracture of the humerus, close to the shoulder, a situation that would require orthopaedic surgery and any number of pins and plates to stabilise.

She asked the nurse to call an orthopaedic specialist, then back in the cubicle worked out what she could fix herself to save the young man extra time under anaesthetic.

She could stitch the gash below his elbow, so, while the nurse flushed the wound with saline to clean out any remaining debris, Kate repeated the checks that the ambulance attendants had already done. Pulse, blood pressure, oxygenation and temperature were all taken then recorded on the man's file. Now she began a more careful examination of him, checking every area of his skin, palpating his stomach, listening to his chest, gently checking for damage to his rib cage.

He seemed all right, although he didn't understand the questions she kept asking, and when the nurse repeated them in the local language, she drew a blank, as well.

'He must be a migrant worker,' the nurse explained. 'There are many hundreds of them in the city.'

'Do we have translators?' Kate asked.

The nurse shook her head.

'They do at the big hospital where he will go for his operation, so he will be all right.'

He would, Kate knew, but she'd have liked to talk to him, even through an intermediary, because only the patient could tell you exactly how he was feeling, and where he had pain.

Could she talk to Fareed about this? Ask if would be possible to have translators here, or would there be too many nationalities concerned?

Perhaps—

'I am Dr Livingstone.'

The man who appeared through the curtain made the announcement as if he was, indeed, the famous African explorer.

Kate had to laugh.

'Kate Andrews,' she said, holding out her hand to the big, bluff, middle-aged man looming over her patient.

'Mike!' Dr Livingstone told her as he shook her hand. 'You've got yourself something you can't handle.'

Kate pointed to the X-rays still in the light boxes on the wall.

'Hmm, nasty one indeed. What's he had?'

Kate listed what she knew.

'I was about to sew up that gash below his elbow,' she explained.

'Not to worry,' Mike told her. 'I'll have one of my lackeys do it while he's under. Okay if we take him now?'

Slightly bewildered by the speed at which things were happening in this very different ER, Kate nodded.

'See you again, then,' Mike said, as he followed the trolley with his patient on it out of the cubicle. 'We have monthly socials at the big hospital and often a group of us will get together for dinner in between. I'll get someone to put your name on the list, and get your contact details from HR so we might see you soon.'

Just what she hadn't wanted to happen—getting dragged into a hospital social scene that, once her relationship to Fareed was known, would lead to never-ending questions and speculation.

Never mind, when an invitation came she could say no.

Would have to say no!

Wouldn't she?

The day continued to be busy, and it was only when she remembered she had to leave to meet her young friends at the mall that Kate realised she'd missed lunch.

She explained to the woman who'd shown her around that she had to go, and asked how she could let her driver know.

'Oh, he'll be waiting for you outside. Once he sees you come out the staff entrance, he'll collect you immediately.'

Kate frowned at the woman.

'You mean he's been sitting there all day, just waiting for me to reappear.'

The woman shrugged.

'It's what drivers do.'

Kate shook her head, unable to believe such things could happen.

'Where are you headed?' her informant asked.

'I'm meeting some friends at the mall,' Kate explained.

'Not with that hair,' her new friend told her. 'Wait, I'll get you a scarf and an *abaya*—there are always spare ones hanging around in the staffroom in case one of the women on the staff decides not to go straight home.'

'Do all women wear them all the time in public?'

The young woman smiled and led her into the staffroom.

'Most of the expats don't, but you're different, aren't you? You're married to our prince and everyone knows you've got red hair so if you want any peace while you're out and about, you'll have to cover up. In here it's okay, our patients will be delighted to think they're being treated by a princess. Stand still, I'll show you how to tie the scarf. You need pins to keep it tight under your chin, then the rest just flows around your shoulders and down your back. Should have put the *abaya* on first, but we'll manage.'

Once clothed from head to toe in black, Kate looked at herself in the mirror.

'The pale skin and glasses are a bit of a giveaway,' she said, but her friend—now introduced as Roberta—shook her head.

'When you're dressed like that you're anonymous. No one will look twice at you.'

Kate thanked her and found her way to the staff

entrance where, as if by osmosis, her driver was pulling in.

And probably not by osmosis, Fareed was looming.

'You do not need to wear that outer clothing to ride back to the palace,' he said, his voice still tight with anger.

'I'm calling in at the mall on the way back,' Kate told him, 'so Roberta suggested I cover up. Is that right?'

It took every ounce of courage she possessed to look directly into his face while she spoke—directly into that anger.

Was she hoping to see it soften?

She didn't know, but a small pain in her chest told her she was sorry this had happened—that she'd lost what little rapport she'd had with him already.

'Why the mall? Is there something you need? You have only to ask one of the servants at the palace and she will fetch it for you.'

'Are you saying I can't go to the mall? That my life will be limited to the hospital and the palace, with perhaps a little sightseeing as a special treat?'

Her own anger was building now, although she remembered claiming it was all she needed.

'I am not saying that at all,' he growled. 'I am just not happy about you going alone to such a place. You should have a maid with you, and a manservant. Anything could happen!'

'At a mall? Anyway, I'm going to meet the girls—the young women—and have a coffee with them. Is that a crime?'

He gave a huff of frustration.

'Of course it's not a crime. Somehow you turn my words against me, but you're a stranger here and my responsibility, I only want that you be safe.'

Seeing him at a loss, her anger vanished and she saw he'd left himself wide-open for a tease.

'That wasn't all you wanted last night with that kiss,' she reminded him, and skipped over to where the ever-patient driver was holding the car door open.

Had Thalia the soothsayer led Ibrahim to this woman knowing she was some kind of witch? Had his uncle chosen her knowing she'd cast some kind of spell over his nephew and drive him to distraction with her behaviour? Thalia had certainly been a presence in the palace prior to the trip to Australia.

He shook his head in disgust at his thoughts.

Thalia wouldn't have known of a witch way out there in Australia.

Not a witch with milk-white skin and glinting green eyes...

Yet in one day at work and she'd defied him, made him look a fool in front of his young cousins and now taunted him and departed before he could hit back.

And there was something going on with those girls, he knew it, and as a man in the family, surely it was his duty to find out what it was.

Kate found the three friends sitting in a coffee shop, behind a screen that provided a private place for women on their own to sit and enjoy each other's company.

Beyond the screen men and women sat together, families with small children, and men with men, some robed in traditional costume, others in western clothes.

Good-looking men, all of them, and the women, even with only their faces visible, were beautiful.

But she wasn't here to talk about the beauty of the local people—

'Have you thought about what you're going to tell your parents?' she asked.

'Why?' Farida asked, and Kate thought about her answer.

'Although it was only a minor incident, and Mai wasn't badly hurt, any attempt at suicide must be reported—well, in my country it must, at least.'

'But we didn't mean it!' they cried in unison.

'Except you thought you did,' Kate reminded them. 'You know now it was silly, and juvenile, and something you just did without thinking, but I do believe you should talk to your parents, all of you. Tell them about the oath you swore when you were too young to understand what death meant, but more than that talk to them about arranged marriage and how you feel about it. I am sure your parents all love you very much, and would not do anything to cause you distress, so talk about these things, and listen to them, as well—listen when they explain why they wish the best for you.'

'They *do* always want the best for us,' Mai said gloomily. 'And they allow us a lot more freedom than some of our friends at college get.'

'So will I come with you now to talk to Farida's parents, then maybe they could arrange for the other parents to join us and we can get it over and done with?'

'But you haven't had a coffee,' Farida objected, and Kate smiled.

'I'd rather go now—putting things off never helps,' she said.

Suley led the way to where her driver was waiting for them. She spoke quietly to him, obviously telling him to take them all to Farida's house.

'Will both your parents be there?' Kate asked, and Farida assured her they would be.

'It is Thursday and my father is always home from the office early.'

The car swept along the esplanade then turned into a high-walled enclave, the ornately carved metal gate swinging open at some electronic command.

Farida's mother greeted Kate warmly, showering praise on how beautiful her guest had looked at her wedding.

Of course these people would have been there, Kate realised, not that she remembered any of the hundreds she had met.

Farida explained Kate had come to talk to both her parents, and one servant was dispatched to bring coffee and cakes, while another was sent to get Farida's father.

'Is this bad?' Farida's mother asked Kate quietly as the friends led the way into a small lounge room.

'Not bad but a little complicated,' Kate told her. 'Silly schoolgirl stuff, really, but something I couldn't not talk to someone about.'

Farida's father arrived and bowed low to Kate, making her feel very uncomfortable, but once they were all settled, it was Farida who took over, kneeling at her father's knee, holding his hand and telling the story from the beginning, blinking back tears at times but going on determinedly.

'Oh, my darling girls,' Farida's mother said, taking Mai in her arms and hugging her, then gathering Suley on her other side, while Farida's father lifted his daughter from the floor and held her on his knee as if she were two years old again.

'Thank you,' he said to Kate. 'You were right to come. I will call the other parents and tell them what has happened, and although all three will be scolded, no harm has been done as long as all three of you swear that you will never do anything so foolish again.'

'And that you will talk to us, or to Dr Kate, if you are troubled by anything,' Farida's mother added.

'There is nothing so bad in all the world that you cannot tell us, is there, Dr Kate?'

Kate shook her head, blinking back her own tears, probably brought on by seeing this close family when her own was so far away.

So far away and living in ignorance of her deceit! The pain of *that* stabbed again and she stood up rather hurriedly.

'I'll leave you with it and be going,' she said, then remembered she'd been driven here with the girls.

'Oh, I left my driver at the mall,' she said, feeling embarrassed by her casual behaviour.

'He will have followed us here,' Mai told her. 'Come on, we'll walk you to the door to make sure he's waiting.'

He was, which didn't make Kate feel any better about not telling him where she'd been going. But when she tried to apologise he waved her words away.

'I will always be waiting for you,' he said, and after her earlier moment of weakness she felt strangely comforted.

'That girl had attempted suicide!'

The accusation hit Kate as she walked into the

suite, surprised to find Fareed there and too weary for an argument.

'And good evening to you, too,' she muttered, slumping tiredly into one of the chairs by the window.

'You should have told me. I must speak to the parents.'

'All done, all fixed,' Kate said, 'and, anyway, it wasn't a serious attempt—she was demonstrating to the others how easy it was to do, then fainted when she realised she'd drawn blood.'

She looked across at Fareed, who was pacing the space beyond the bed.

'And I refrained from telling them that if they were serious about wrist slitting as a means of suicide they should cut long ways along the vein, not across where the tendons protected it.'

He halted on the spot and stared at her, so much disbelief on his face that Kate had to laugh.

'Joke, Fareed, joke!'

'It is not funny, such things are very serious. Suicide is a crime in my country.'

'Mine, too, I think,' Kate told him, then, not wanting to get into another argument with him, she shook off her lethargy and stood up. 'I think I'll have a swim.'

She opened her mouth to ask him to join her then closed it again, imagining just how much trouble she'd be in with this man almost naked in the water beside her, the sensual slither of water on skin magnifying the silly attraction she had towards him.

'I'll join you,' he said, startling her so much by this about-face from angry man to companion that she almost decided against the idea. He'd disappeared into his dressing room, and she made her way more slowly into hers, thinking about the cool, revivifying water—and droplets of it on tanned skin...

He had to do something about his impulse control, Fareed decided as he shut the door on the woman who seemed determined to torment him.

He'd always prided himself on control, but just lately it appeared to have taken a holiday.

Or he'd taken leave of his senses!

He should get out of this place—go for a drive or, better still, a ride.

A memory of a woman on a horse flashed through his mind.

He burst back into the bedroom of the suite, crossing to the door into Kate's dressing room, knocking, then opening it slightly to call through the gap.

'Will a swim suffice this evening or would you like to go for a ride? There's a full moon rising early so even if we go too far, we'll have moonlight on our return.'

Riding by moonlight? In that magical desert?

Kate tossed her swimsuit back into the cupboard.

'Give me five minutes,' she said, as she pulled old jeans and a checked shirt out of the cupboard, then searched through what seemed like dozens of pairs of sandals for her boots.

'Thank you, Fareed,' she said, as she met him in the bedroom. 'This will be much better than a swim.'

Partly because our near-naked bodies won't be frolicking closely in the sensual water, but also because there's nothing as good as a ride for blowing the cobwebs from the brain, and allowing it to think more clearly.

And her brain certainly needed to do that.

He'd been waiting for her, dressed much as she was, but projecting such arrogant masculinity she had to restrain her body from flinging itself at him.

'Beach or desert?' he asked, as he led her along

a now more familiar corridor towards the rear of the palace.

'Beach or desert?' she echoed.

Her bewilderment must have been evident in her voice for he turned and smiled.

The smile had even more effect on her body than the sight of him had earlier—the man was sex personified.

'To ride—the beach or the desert?'

'Oh!' Kate managed, swallowing hard and hoping her errant thoughts had been swallowed at the same time. 'Desert for sure. Maybe the beach some other time, but I've never ridden in a desert. How do the horses manage in the soft sand?' *Good work, Kate, you sound almost normal.* 'I know camels have specially developed hooves but horses?'

He turned away again and she hurried to catch up.

'The sand is good for their hooves and very good for strengthening their legs.'

Duh!

'Of course, I did know that,' Kate said, remembering the countless times her parents had taken horses to the beach—taken her along, as well, as a rider on the string. It was just that Fareed's presence was causing brain melt.

Or she hoped that's all it was!

A stablehand was holding the bridle on the stallion whose head she'd glimpsed over a stall, while a smaller boy held a saddled gelding, a dark grey-black, and possibly the most beautiful horse Kate had ever seen.

'Oh, you beauty,' she whispered, as she walked quietly towards it, holding out her hand so the horse could check on the stranger.

'He's very well behaved,' Fareed said, and Kate wondered if he'd added 'unlike some women' under his breath.

Moving automatically, Kate checked the gear, sliding her fingers beneath the girth to make sure it hadn't loosened. Satisfied, she put a foot in the stirrup and vaulted into the saddle, happiness flooding through her at the familiarity of a horse beneath her.

'Oh, Fareed,' she said, 'this is so much better than a swim.'

'You haven't gone anywhere yet,' he reminded her, but she thought she detected that little smile she'd seen before—a smile he didn't really want to smile…

He swung easily into the stallion's saddle and led the way sedately out of the yard, across a big training paddock behind the stables, through a wide iron gate held open by a wizened old man, and straight from grassy field to desert, the sand painted red by the setting sun.

The stallion was prancing, held on a tight rein but obviously ready to take off.

'He needs a run. I'll go ahead and come back when he's shaken out his fidgets,' Fareed told her, and Kate nodded, her breath stolen by the sight of the man she'd married astride the powerful, cavorting animal with the red glow of the sunset behind them.

He swung the horse around and took off, the stallion streaking across the soft sand. Kate's horse pranced now, wanting to join the action, but, not knowing the animal, she started slowly, getting the feel of him as he trotted then cantered and finally stretched his legs in a full gallop, following some path only he could see towards the other horse and rider.

Fareed rode back to meet her, and they moved at

a more sedate pace towards a high outcrop of rock. As they drew closer, Kate made out the shape of a building at the top.

'Is that the old fort?' she asked. 'It looks different from this side.'

'Would you like to see it? We can ride there.'

Kate turned towards the man who rode beside her, wondering just how much of this togetherness she could take. But her interest in the old building overcame the warnings her head was offering—warnings about spending too much time with Fareed—too much 'friendly' time…

'I'd love to see it,' she said, and although she meant the words, she still felt a shiver down her spine—as if by committing to the destination she was moving into the unknown.

'Race you to that palm tree,' she challenged, in an attempt to clear her mind of fancies she didn't understand. It was also a good idea because his horse was so much faster she'd be spared his proximity for a little while.

Maybe that would help her sort out what was going on her body.

And her mind!

He'd beaten her easily, but Fareed turned so he

could watch her, see the effortless way she rode, at one with the animal, strands of red hair flying loose from its restraining plait.

He imagined that hair splayed across a pillow—a pillow next to his—and his body quickened. Would a physical relationship be possible?

He knew he wanted it, but Kate—Katya as he now thought of her... Of her feelings, he had no idea, although she *had* responded to his kisses— responded with a fire as vibrant as her hair.

But she *had* married him for money, which made everything she did and said suspect. A woman who'd accept a bribe like that would do anything for money—or so he imagined.

She pulled up, flushed and laughing.

'That was wonderful,' she said, breathing deeply to slow her heart rate. 'Just wonderful!'

And all aglow like that, she was almost...

Beautiful?

She put herself down over her looks, but—

'Well,' she said, while he was still trying to work out why the sight of her flushed and panting had affected him so deeply, 'are we going on to the fort?'

The sky was streaked with the last colours of the fading day, but the track to the fort was wide and well marked and by the time they came down the moon would be out.

'If that is what you'd like,' he said, uncertain now that spending even more time with her was a good idea.

She studied him for a moment, then smiled and said, 'It definitely is!'

Now she was smiling as well as looking almost beautiful. He led the way around the hill to where the track began, but his mind was on the woman following him—the woman who had been paid to be his wife—and why he was suddenly feeling very confused about her.

Kate's horse picked its way delicately up the track, allowing her time to sit and admire the broad shoulders, slim hips and straight back of the rider in front of her.

Was this little adventure a good idea or a bad one? By the time they returned and ate dinner it would be late and she could plead tiredness and re-tire to bed, although maybe he wouldn't be around, wouldn't eat dinner with her, so there'd be no danger of them taking those kisses they'd shared any further.

And surely that wasn't disappointment squelching away inside her?

Did she actually *want* to get sexually involved with this man?

Wouldn't that just complicate matters too much?

And how could she separate out sexual feelings and emotional feelings? Could she have sex with someone she didn't love?

Wouldn't there have to be an element of love somewhere in there for the sex to be enjoyable?

And surely enjoyable sex and love weren't all that far apart...

CHAPTER NINE

'TAKE CARE ON this corner,' Fareed said, and Kate turned her mind from sex and love to concentrating on her horse.

Although once around the corner, she paused and looked around, amazed at how close the shoreline was, edging the red desert sands that flowed from the mountain.

'It's fantastic,' she said. 'I really have to get a map and drive around so I can orient myself. From here, you'd never know there was a city out there. It's so peaceful and serene, so untouched somehow.'

'The desert, like the ocean, is forever renewing itself. It is little wonder my forbears, seeing how this happened, believed life could do that too—believed in an afterlife in which you were rewarded for the good you did on earth.'

Kate nodded, looking into Fareed's dark eyes, aware how easy it would be to drown in them—liking him far more than she'd admit even to herself in case liking led to love and this was a bargain with a time limitation, not a real marriage.

He'd moved his horse towards the rocky edge of the track and she drew up beside him so they could look out together.

'The desert is my past,' he said quietly, 'the past that is in my blood. But although it's hidden from us now, the city does exist.'

He turned towards her, the reins loose in his hands, which rested on the stallion's neck.

'That city, Kate, is the future, although my people are ill prepared for it.'

He sighed, and Kate stayed silent, willing him to keep speaking, wanting to learn more of this man she didn't know.

'Ibrahim is doing his best, but his roots are more deeply buried in the desert, so seeing to the transition, getting it right, will be my job.'

'You make is sound like an enormous burden,' Kate said quietly, and he smiled at her.

'Only when I'm looking at the desert and thinking of the freedom it offers, or when I'm on this beauty and feeling the freedom of his stride.'

He patted the stallion's neck.

'Could no one else do the job?' Kate asked, hearing the pain in his voice as he spoke. 'You already run the hospital and work there many hours past your roster. Does Ibrahim not have sons who could take over?'

Fareed shook his head.

'My father was the eldest brother, so it is my duty,' he said, 'and one I will one day take it on with pride, but it worries me how best to help my people move forward. The hospital was a trial run, you might say. There I've been putting some of my ideas to work, employing as many women as possible in an effort to bring in some gender equality—but, on the other hand, I want the people, our patients, to accept this equality. You were right to point out there are times when it is appropriate to see a doctor of one's own sex, but for a cut toe or a headache? Surely whatever doctor is available should do?'

'But the people don't see it that way?'

He turned from the desert to look directly at her.

'I think it must be something in our blood—the blood of our men—that we are so protective of our women. Here I am, a modern man, yet when I saw you in that *abaya* I wanted to forbid you to go to the mall, or at the least send a phalanx of guards along with you.'

Kate laughed and touched his arm.

'All change takes time, you must know that,' she said gently, but he didn't reply, simply turning his horse back onto the track and riding on.

Kate's horse followed closely, while she considered this side of Fareed she'd never seen. She couldn't help but feel empathy for this man who longed for freedom yet was bound by duty to his people, chained by the need to do his best for them at what was obviously a very difficult time.

They rounded another bend and there was the fort. An earth-coloured building, looking as if it had grown out of the rock, it had the same air of permanence as the rock itself. An outer courtyard was lit by lamps hung along the walls, and carpets were spread across it.

'People live here, then?' she asked, remembering something Fareed had said about it but not the details.

'A caretaker and his family are permanent residents, and sometimes artists and artisans stay here while they are doing restoration work. The only vehicle here now is the caretaker's so maybe it's just his family at the moment.'

He waved his hand towards a decrepit old four-wheel drive parked in one corner of the courtyard, then dismounted and turned to hold Kate's horse while she swung off.

She straightened up, moving her feet and shaking off a little stiffness while Fareed led the horses to a corner and hitched their bridles on a rail above a trough of water.

'Come,' he called to Kate, and she crossed a faded, sandy carpet towards a door that opened into the largest of the round towers she'd seen from the car that first morning. It was set at one end of a long, low building.

'This was the main lookout tower but it was also the quarters for the headman of the village and his family when the village was raided from the sea.'

Inside, lamplight threw strange shadows on the spiral stairs that curved up out of sight. To the right of the staircase, an open arch led into a round room, made smaller on one side by the staircase. On the other side, a long, thin window let in the last of the daylight.

Fareed flicked a switch and lamps around the walls lit the room with an amber glow.

'When I was a child, we still used oil lamps when we came here—my uncle and cousins and friends. It was a great adventure then, to play games by lamplight and snuggle under rugs to sleep by the light of the one lamp that stayed lit.'

He sounded more sad than nostalgic and Kate fought an urge to put her arm around him and give him a quick hug. He'd walked to the window and was looking out, and she lost the fight.

She followed him, standing beside him and slipping her arm around his shoulders as she asked, 'Your uncle and cousins? Did your parents never come?'

She felt him stiffen and withdrew her arm, embarrassed by her action, moving away, back to the opening, changing the subject as quickly as she could.

'Does the staircase go to the top?'

He was still at the window, staring out, lost, she imagined, in the past.

But was he in the happy past of camping out in the tower with friends, or some unhappy past her question had revived?

Oh, bother him! she decided, and began to climb the stairs. A landing and another arched door, another room inside the arch, then up again, this time to the top, a terrace surrounded by battlements, but no longer a place of war because half of it was shaded by a frame that held up filmy draperies, making an elaborate gazebo, open on one side, to reveal carpets and piles of cushions—a party place or just a place of peace and beauty where people could relax.

But the battlements drew her first, and she crossed to one of the slits in the high stone walls and peered out, pleased to see the sea, dark now, with just the silver wash of foam on the little waves that broke upon the beach.

She felt him before she heard him—felt his presence right behind her—then his hand slid around her shoulders as hers had earlier held his.

'I'm sorry. My family—close family—was dysfunctional, to say the least. Ibrahim and his wife brought me up with their children so all my good memories are of times I shared with them.'

Kate moved so she rested against his body.

'I'm the one who's sorry, hurting you with an unthinking question. My family has been my life, and after seeing Farida with her family today I imagined family was just as important here as it is at home.'

'It is,' he said, holding her closer. 'But nothing's ever perfect, is it?'

He turned her slightly, looked down into her face for a moment, then his head bent and his lips touched hers, igniting all the nerves he'd awoken in her the previous night.

It's just a kiss, she told herself, but herself took no notice, responding as if it was an invitation to whatever wild and wonderful sex he might propose.

The kiss deepened, stole her breath, had her melting against him, then cool air brushed her lips and he was gone, striding to another part of the roof, peering out into the darkening night.

Fareed closed his eyes to the beauty and tried to make sense of his actions.

They'd been talking about his family yet still he'd kissed this paid-for wife of his—the woman who was no better than his mother.

Kissed her until she'd responded…

He could hardly say she was seducing him when it was he initiating the kisses.

And wanting more!

He ached for her, something that was very new and strange in his contained and controlled lifestyle.

Was this how his father had felt?

It *had* to be some genetic code written into them that made them fools over women with red hair…

And Ibrahim—did he know this? Had he chosen Kate for that reason?

And now he, Fareed, had spoiled their time together—spoiled the small adventure that she had begun with such delight, as if he'd handed her a very special gift.

He walked back to where she stood, still looking out to sea, and took her hand, turning her so she faced him.

'Are you hungry? Do you want to go back for dinner, or could we sit and talk a little?'

The moon was rising but its light was not strong enough for him to read her face.

She was silent for a moment, then nodded.

'Yes, perhaps talking would be good.'

He led her to the cushioned retreat beneath the silken curtains and held her hand to support her as she settled amongst them.

Held her hand when they were both seated, close but not touching, apart from her hand in his.

'My mother was a foreigner,' he began. 'My father was besotted with her, but she hated Amberach and used any excuse to get away from it. The only time I saw her was on her rare visits to the palace.'

'She didn't take you with her when she left?'

Kate had moved so she could see his face when he answered, but the little tent was shadowed so reading it was impossible—or maybe that should be more impossible than usual!

Fareed sighed and his grip on her fingers tightened.

'That could have been my father's fault—he might have insisted I stay here.'

'You don't sound as if you believe that.'

Another sigh, deeper than the last.

'I don't, not for one minute!'

The words were blunt, but Kate heard hurt behind them—hurt and anger.

Pain caused by a red-haired foreigner, Kate realised, remembering the women's chat at the henna party!

'Oh, Fareed,' she whispered, and she slipped her free hand around his neck and held him close.

The kiss, she realised later, had been inevitable, as had been all that had followed it. The touches, the exploration, the building excitement that had turned to hot, ferocious need and the furious, winner-take-all coupling that had left them lying exhausted, entwined and breathless, but holding hard to each other as if they needed anchorage to the earth.

'I'll never find my clothes,' Kate grumbled, not moving from within Fareed's arms.

'Are you in such a hurry to move away from me that you need your clothes?'

There was a hint of laughter in Fareed's voice and Kate responded by snuggling closer.

'I suppose it's being naked or near naked in a strange place,' she said, murmuring the words against the satiny skin on his shoulder, licking at it when she'd done talking.

'Keep doing that and you won't need clothes for a while longer,' he growled, but Kate knew they had to move. Down in the courtyard the horses were waiting, and her stomach was telling her it needed dinner.

But what did this mean?

Would this Fareed, who'd shared more of himself than his body, ride home with her, eat dinner with her, sleep in the same bed as her, or were they back to being polite strangers—colleagues?

She moved and found her clothes, pulling them back on, wondering why she'd thought a ride with her husband would be less likely to end in sex than the two of them swimming together.

The ride home was magical, the moon now throwing its silvery light across the desert so Kate felt as if they rode across the sea; the dunes were waves so the sea was solid, but so serene and beautiful, she wondered how anyone could not fall in love with this fantastic country.

They were handing their horses over to stable hands when Fareed's mobile rang.

He answered it, turning from her and walking away slightly, talking English, but she couldn't hear the words.

Finishing the call, he turned back towards her and raised his hands in a helpless gesture.

'I have to go back to the hospital. One of the duty doctors has gone home ill.'

'Do you need me? I could come,' Kate said, but

the Fareed she barely knew and definitely couldn't read was back and he thanked her politely, led her back to their suite, then said goodbye.

He wouldn't have wished his colleague ill, but the phone call had been a lifesaver, Fareed decided as he made his way to the hospital. He'd had no idea how to proceed as far as his marriage was concerned.

He knew it for a sham, despised the fact that Kate—she was only Katya in his other thoughts—had married him for money, and he was still determined not to become emotionally involved with her.

That had been his father's problem—fancying himself totally in love with a woman who had only had eyes for the money she could suck out of him—a beautiful flame-haired leech.

Yet every instinct told him Kate—Katya, anyway—was different, although that might be part of the ensnarement.

Al'ama! What was he to do?

Put aside the problem of the woman and concentrate on your work, the sensible, and obviously nonsensual side of his brain told him, but could he?

He'd work it out tomorrow!

* * *

Kate pressed one of the buttons that summoned a servant and asked if she could have dinner served in half an hour.

After the hospitable companionship of eating with the other women before her wedding, this seemed weird to say the least, and she hoped they wouldn't think she was avoiding them.

But she had no idea what she should be doing— whether she should be seeking them out.

Except that might make them think Fareed was neglecting her.

Oh, hell and damnation, was nothing easy?

She showered, and emerged to find her dinner waiting, a tray full of delicious-looking dishes, ice cream in a wide cooler and a bowl of fruit.

Had they sent enough for both her and Fareed? It certainly looked that way.

And when she'd barely eaten half of it, what would the servants think? What gossip would ensue?

Bother this! She'd eat her dinner, send some emails—including a long one to Billy about the horses and the fort and the desert—then go to bed and tomorrow she'd have a long talk to Fareed about just what was expected of her in her role as his wife.

Would she be isolated like this for ever?

Or would she be shunted into the women's part of the palace—she already knew it reasonably well—and only see her husband when he…?

Tomorrow!

She'd sort it out tomorrow!

She slept in the big bed, woke early and alone, and decided to have a swim before breakfast. The ritual of pushing buttons to summon servants was still strange and uncomfortable for her, but she pushed a button anyway, ordered breakfast in an hour, then asked the young woman to tell her driver she'd be leaving for the hospital a half-hour after that.

Would this kind of thing ever become 'normal'? Kate doubted it, at least not in a year, which was all she'd promised Ibrahim she'd stay.

And why did thinking about that promise cause anxiety in her stomach, a kind of cold dismay?

It was the limit of a year—she knew that. Less than a year now that she'd share with Fareed? Barely time to get to know him—yet time enough to fall in love?

Last night, at the top of the tower at the old fort, it had felt like love, lying with him, listening to talk of his childhood, his mother, hearing his pain…

He was at the hospital when she arrived, already doing a handover to one of the other doctors coming on duty.

The smile he greeted her with was tired, but even a tired smile set her heart thumping in her chest.

'I will see you later—I'll go home and sleep and be back this afternoon,' he said, walking with her to the staff room where she could drop her bag.

'You're all right? Not too busy a night?' Kate asked, while inside she was cursing herself for the pathetic conversation. This man was her *husband*, for heaven's sake! Okay, so over here she couldn't hug or kiss him in public, but shouldn't their conversation be easier?

Less forced?

'A pretty good night. The only busy time was when some young men, joy-riding, as they do, wiped out their car on a roundabout. One's in hospital up the road, head and spinal injuries, but the others were lucky and escaped with only assorted broken limbs and bumps and bruises.'

'Which would have kept you busy for quite some time,' Kate guessed, and was rewarded with another smile, a better effort this time, but they were talking work, so he probably felt smiling at her was safe.

'It did,' he said, holding the door open for her.

Kate slipped inside and was surprised when he followed, dropped a kiss on her cheek, squeezed her shoulders, then said, 'I'll see you later.'

Boy, oh, boy! A kiss on the cheek and I've gone weak-kneed!

She stood in the staff room, holding the palm of her hand to the cheek he'd kissed, and felt like an idiot. It was obviously too late to decide not to fall in love with him.

The morning was quiet apart from one man refusing to be treated by a woman for a nasty wound on his hand, and one woman whose husband insisted she only be seen by a woman.

Another pregnant patient! This one had had a fall, and both of them were beside themselves in case the fall had done some damage to the baby.

Kate helped the woman onto an examination table and sat the man on a chair.

'The baby's really well protected in there,' she assured them. 'He or she is floating around in a sac of fluid that's a bit like airbags in a car, designed to protect the occupant. But I will check your wife, and the baby's heartbeat, and then, if you wish, do a scan to check on the baby. You've had a scan before?'

The man shook his head.

'No photographs.'

Not rudely said, but definite.

'That's okay. We did it all before the machines were invented, there's no reason why we can't do our checking without them now.'

Questions about where and how the woman had fallen provided little information.

'She just fell,' the man said bluntly, and a shiver down Kate's spine suggested domestic abuse.

But the man seemed genuinely concerned for his wife and the wife very dependent on him, shaking her head rather than speaking, so Kate set it aside.

'Do you know how pregnant your wife is?' she asked the man.

'Twenty-two weeks,' he said with no hesitation, giving Kate a base from which to work in her examination.

'Has she had any bleeding?'

The man shook his head, looking so embarrassed, Kate found herself believing him.

Pulse, blood pressure…

Uncertain about the protocol of baring a woman's arm, she wrapped the blood-pressure cuff around the fine material of the woman's tunic.

The machine puffed and clicked, the eventual reading one hundred and eight over seventy. Given that blood pressure dropped in early pregnancy, and picked up towards the middle, this was almost clinically perfect. Pulse and respirations were also good and when she worked out the mean arterial pressure, it also came out perfect.

Now she asked the woman, who'd been sitting on the table, to lie down on her back. Kate put her arm around her to help ease her down, but the husband took over and as he settled his wife on the table the gentleness in his hands and the anxiety in his eyes told Kate he genuinely loved this woman.

The nurse, who'd been standing quietly at the end of the cubicle, stepped forward with a small sheet to cover the woman, and Kate spread it across her belly and legs.

Kate reached beneath it for the bottom of the woman's tunic, ready to lift it then ease down the trousers, so she could listen to the baby's heart, but she'd no sooner touched the cloth than the man rose from his seat again.

'Do not touch her clothes. You must do what you do through clothes.'

So why did you want a woman doctor? she thought, but she obediently felt around her patient's body, seeking any sore spots from the fall. The woman gasped when Kate touched the right hip.

'She fell on her hip?' she asked the man, accepting he was the voice of the patient.

'On the step outside. It must have been wet and she slipped.'

'I imagine there's quite a bruise. I can give you something to rub on it to ease it. Now I'll listen to the baby's heart.'

But not through a sheet and her tunic and her trousers.

The nurse handed Kate a Pinard's stethoscope, something she hadn't seen for many years, but right now, in these circumstances when she couldn't press a foetoscope to the woman's distended belly, it would be ideal.

She pressed the wide end to the clothing, carefully put her ear to it, then removed her hands so her own heartbeats wouldn't interfere with what she heard.

Definite heartbeats, faint and rapid. The faintness she put down to listening through layers of clothing and the rapidity was normal. She moved it around, heard nothing to worry about and lifted her head.

'It all sounds good,' she told the woman. 'Are you feeling movement?'

The woman spoke for the first time, not to Kate but to her husband.

'She said the baby kicked when you put that instrument on her belly. She said the baby didn't like it but she is pleased because the baby hadn't been moving and now it is.'

He was beaming at Kate, as if somehow she'd performed a miracle.

'Take her home, but make sure she rests for a few days,' Kate told him, 'and if you are worried about anything, come back.'

'You will always see her?' the man asked.

'Perhaps not, but there will always be a woman doctor on duty, and you must have a regular doctor—are you seeing an obstetrician?'

The man nodded.

'But she is busy-busy, only one woman doing

this in Amberach, so very hard to get in to see her without an appointment.'

He had helped his wife to her feet and was now guiding her out of the cubicle, his arm around her shoulders.

Kate asked the nurse to find a jar of arnica for the bruising, and with repeated thanks, the pair departed.

Later, Kate decided, she'd have to have a long talk to Fareed about customs and protocols for dealing with the locals. In fact, shouldn't she have had a proper orientation tour and talk, rather than a nurse showing her around?

Her life seemed to be straying farther and farther from any known path and while she wasn't willing to believe it was completely off track, she had no idea what track it might be taking.

CHAPTER TEN

FAREED WOKE IN his apartment at the hospital, answered a dozen messages waiting on his phone, then decided it was time to think about his situation—his marriage.

What was going on that he was so drawn to this woman—physically drawn?

Would a psychologist put it down to his longing for some mother love? Was it as simple as that?

But he wouldn't have wanted to be racing his mother off to bed, so surely that wasn't right!

This morning, as he'd walked Katya to the staff room and followed her inside, he'd had an almost overwhelming urge to kiss her properly, although he'd known full well where kissing her would inevitably have led.

He'd even had the notion that the door had a lock on it flash through his head.

He *could* put it down to tiredness, this morning's episode, but last night at the fort?

Part of his brain told him not to let it worry him, the woman was his wife, it was natural he should enjoy sex with her, but enjoy hardly covered it, and was it natural to *crave* sex with her?

He clasped his hands to his head and squeezed hard—hoping to squeeze out memories of delight?

To squeeze out answers?

The demanding beeping of his phone saved him from further soul-searching and frustration.

Suley's mother, asking if he and Kate would have dinner with them that evening.

'Farida and Mai will be here, and their parents, of course. We would like to thank your wife for the sensible way she handled the girls and have a talk to them with both of you present if that is all right.'

Fareed agreed, while at the same time wondering just what Kate had handled.

All fixed, she'd said to him and nothing more, changing the topic of conversation by talking of a swim, which had turned into a ride, which had—

No, he was over the soul-searching, for a while at least. Best he get back and find Kate—or Katya?—to tell her about this evening.

She was talking to Roberta, the English nurse who had been here since the hospital opened.

'Kate's just had a pregnant patient whose husband refused to let Kate remove clothes to listen to the foetal heartbeat.' Roberta was smiling. 'I told her your stories of the old days when doctors were supposed to diagnose what was wrong with women by looking at a hand, or even one finger, the only part of the woman's body the husband would allow the doctor to see.'

Fareed smiled back.

'Times are changing but we cannot hurry change. It was a win for us that the man brought his wife here.' He turned to Kate. 'Do you think if you'd asked him to put the stethoscope on his wife's belly while you turned your head but listened—would that have worked?'

The two women seemed to be considering it.

'It might have worked,' Kate said, 'but I would have had to be standing very close to him—possibly our bodies touching—and he might not have liked that.'

She was good, this wife of his, Fareed conceded mentally. She seemed genuinely concerned not just for the patient's physical health but for his or her cultural sensibilities.

'I haven't done a lot of midwifery,' she was saying now, 'but do you have those monitors used on women having an induction or in labour—the ones with two discs, one measuring the contractions and the other the foetal heartbeat? They just trace a line on a screen, not a picture—would that work?'

Kate looked directly at Fareed for the first time since he'd joined them—looked and thought she saw a softening in his usually stern face.

Or perhaps that was nothing more than wishful thinking...

'We do not do inductions here but we have at least one of those for emergency admissions when a woman is in labour,' he was saying, and, no, she hadn't been wrong, he was actually smiling at her. 'I'll get someone to show you where—in fact, maybe tomorrow I can ask someone to cover for me and give you a proper orientation.'

It was basic medical talk and exactly what she knew she needed, so why did the words sound suggestive to her—make her insides squirm just slightly?

'In the meantime,' he continued, oblivious of her reaction to his words, 'we need to be getting home. Suley's parents have invited us for dinner, with the other girls and their parents.'

Kate knew she was probably frowning as she looked at him this time.

'I do hope I haven't got you into any trouble,' she said, ignoring Roberta's almost palpable interest.

Another smile from Fareed!

'On the contrary, apparently the dinner is in your honour, to thank you for sorting out something with the girls.'

Relief swept through Kate, although it was not quite enough to cover her trepidation over going to a private dinner with Fareed.

'You are bothered?' he asked as they walked towards the staff room so she could collect her handbag.

'Only because I've got no idea how I'm supposed to behave at a private dinner.' She stopped and looked at him. 'In fact, I've no idea how I'm supposed to behave anywhere, or any time.'

She would have asked more, except the smile was gone and a frown had taken its place. It didn't bother her as she was far more used to his frowns than his smiles, and his frowns didn't make her twitchy inside.

'Did Ibrahim not appoint someone to teach you

some of our ways—at least instruct you in the marriage rituals?'

Kate shook her head.

'Everyone was very kind and they told me things about the clothes to wear and talked about the food as we ate together, but I suppose...'

'Suppose what?' Fareed demanded.

Kate's courage wavered but in the end held firm.

'I suppose they thought that you would tell me anything I needed to know.'

She knew she was blushing, probably from her chest up to her scalp, but he *had* asked.

'Of course!' he said shortly, then he put his hand on her elbow and steered her out of the building. Her driver drew up but Fareed waved him away, leading Kate into a large car park hidden behind shrubs and bushes.

He steered her towards his big black SUV and opened the door for her, again taking her arm to help her into it.

'Ibrahim has used you shamefully,' he muttered as he drove out of the hospital. 'I thought he'd done badly by me, but you! He hands you a pile of money to marry me then leaves you to fend for yourself without any instruction or information or even help.'

'He didn't hand me a pile of money!'

The words were out before Kate could stop them, but that hadn't been the point so she continued with what she'd been going to say. 'And, anyway, he's always busy. He worked on the plane, worrying all the time about things he had to do, and on top of that I don't think he's very well. I think your ana-phylactic shock shocked him more than it shocked you. I think it made him realise how vulnerable we all are and that it was time to get his affairs in order.'

Fareed had pulled over to the side of the road as she'd been talking, and was now studying her intently.

'He *didn't* give you a pile of money?'

Kate waved the question aside. 'We had a bar-gain, something else,' she said, 'but it's Ibrahim you should be thinking about, not me. I haven't seen him since before the wedding but even on the plane coming over, I felt he was unwell. And the day I did see him, not long before we were mar-ried, I thought he was a bad colour, a little sallow, like a hepatitis patient. Are you his doctor?'

Fareed was frowning at her—again—but this time it was more a puzzled frown than an angry one.

'What kind of bargain?' he asked, and Kate wanted to scream with frustration.

'Will you just get off that subject and talk to me about Ibrahim? Don't you care that he might be ill? Do you know who looks after him if you don't? When did you last see him?'

Fareed could have answered easily. He hadn't seen his uncle to talk to properly for weeks. Ibrahim had been busy—busy avoiding his nephew, Fareed now realised—since the wedding, and he'd been angry, and now it wasn't money—

No, he had to stop thinking about that, and consider what Kate was telling him.

Could Ibrahim be ill?

Had he rushed Fareed into marriage thinking the sultan needed a wife and that Fareed would be Sultan sooner than he realised?

'I'll go and see him now,' he announced as he put the car into gear and drew back onto the road. 'There'll be time before we go to dinner.'

The drove home in silence, each lost in their own world of thought.

Once back at the palace, Fareed escorted Kate to the door of their suite and paused to say, 'Convention says we should spend forty days and nights in the suite, but you need not worry about it. You are free to go wherever you wish.'

'Except if I join the women for evening meals, say, they will wonder what is happening in our marriage.'

He nodded.

'Later,' he promised, 'we will talk about it later, but please believe I would rather put up with gossip than have you feeling imprisoned and alienated in my land.'

And to Kate's surprise he kissed her cheek, just as he had when he'd left her in the staff room earlier in the day. Only this time she refused to put her hand across the bit of kissed skin—bad enough to be silly over something even once in a day!

She crossed to the window and looked out at the little courtyard. She could hardly be in a more luxurious prison, and did she really want to be mixing with the other women?

She was still standing there when Fareed returned.

'Ibrahim isn't in but I spoke to his private servant, who assures me he is well. I'll see Ibrahim himself in the morning.'

'That's good,' Kate said, then felt she had to explain. 'I don't feel imprisoned, but not knowing the customs I wondered if the women would think I was being rude not joining them. Now I know, I'm only too happy to go to and from the hospital and to have my meals on my own here. It's such a beautiful and peaceful place—who would not be happy, staying here?'

'My mother!' Fareed said shortly, then he crossed the room, opened the door to his dressing room and disappeared.

The door opened again a few seconds later.

'We'll leave in an hour,' he added, and once again closed the door behind him.

His mother must certainly be one of the ghosts Ibrahim had spoken of, but wasn't having another redhead hanging around the same rooms more likely to bring the ghosts back than banish them?

Kate decided she had no idea, so she headed for her dressing room, determined to find an outfit Suley had given her before the wedding.

It was pink, a colour most redheads avoided, but Kate had loved it from the moment she'd seen it.

Rusty red embroidery—the colour of her hair—
wove intricate patterns around the neck and hem
of the tunic and along the bottom of the trousers,
while the fine material caressed the skin, making
her feel sensually alive.

Possibly not a good when she was going out with
Fareed…

Especially Fareed in local dress—the first time
she'd seen him dressed this way since he'd escorted
her off her stage on their wedding day, and back
then, without her glasses, he'd been nothing more
than a tall, fuzzy figure clad in white and gold.

He wore a long white—dazzlingly white—robe
and over it a kind of full-length vest, the edges
trimmed with two inches of delicate gold embroidery that matched the gold cords he wore to keep
his headdress in place.

'Oh, my!' Kate said, unable to stop staring at the
vision in front of her.

Not that he noticed her wide-eyed amazement,
because he, in turn, was staring at her.

'You look stunning,' he finally said, his voice
gravelly with emotion.

'Same to you,' Kate whispered, still too overawed

to move—to go towards him and the door. 'So different, so regal—you look magnificent.'

He smiled, which all but finished Kate. Her knees went weak, and nerves danced through her body, her brain sending heat to her nipples and lower to between her thighs.

'Shall we go?'

Obviously Fareed was more in control than she was, but she forced herself to move, one step at a time, towards the picture-book prince who awaited her.

A drive took them along the esplanade that ran below the fort and through an open gate into a complex almost as big as the palace. Only this one was made up of many houses—huge houses.

'As each son marries, he builds himself a house, usually larger than his brother's,' Fareed explained.

'So they live as families in their own homes?'

'They do—it's the modern way—but the houses still have some rooms that are for women and some for men—we haven't been entirely westernised as yet.'

Kate heard a smile in the words and wondered whether, if this had been a normal marriage, Fareed would have built a house for her.

'Would you like a house of your own—one you could run as you wish?' he asked, as if her thoughts had flashed through the air into his head.

'I doubt I'd run it properly,' she told him. 'Telling servants what to do is way beyond my comfort zone and probably beyond my capabilities.'

'But you manage it at the palace.'

The car had stopped outside one of the huge houses so Kate felt she didn't have to answer, but although the driver was now holding the door open for them to alight, Fareed remained seated at her side.

'Well?' he prompted.

She tried to find the words she needed, not wanting to sound rude or to offend him.

'There, it's different,' she said. 'I really have no choice, do I? I mean, if I want to eat I have to press the bell and ask a servant to bring me food, but I look at it like room service at a hotel.'

'Something temporary?'

The question held a hint of steel and Kate was flummoxed.

'Not really,' she told him, 'but it's kind of what I was saying earlier—I feel I'm in a situation where I don't know the rules.'

To her surprise he kissed her lightly on the cheek—three in one day?—then climbed out of the car, reaching back to take her hand and help her out.

'For someone who doesn't know the rules you're doing very well,' he told her, just as Suley, Mai and Farida came running down the stairs to welcome them, kissing Fareed on both cheeks then hugging Kate and kissing her, as well.

'Come in and meet my parents,' Suley said, taking her by the hand and leading her up the stairs, pausing while they slipped off their sandals, then directing her into the house, which seemed even larger than it had looked from the outside.

'Last brother to marry?' she whispered to Fareed as he caught up with them and took her free hand.

He nodded, and smiled, and Kate's heart leapt in her chest, ignoring all her warnings that she shouldn't fall in love with this man. After all, she was only here for a year and to leave him if she loved him…

They were led into a huge reception room, to where the three sets of parents waited in a grouping of comfortable armchairs and lounges about halfway down the room.

Introductions done, they were offered cool drinks and appetisers, tiny nibbles of food so delicious Kate would have been happy to make it dinner.

Suley's father sat beside her and took her hand as he thanked her formally for taking care of the three silly young women.

'We had no idea such adolescent fantasies still lingered in their heads,' Suley's mother said. 'They should all have known that even if we suggest someone we think would make a suitable husband for them, these days they will have the opportunity to meet him and decide for themselves. We are not so strict about such things as some people.'

'Of course, they would be chaperoned at these meetings,' Mai's father put in. 'That protects their reputation, but none of us would want our daughters to be unhappy so we would never force them to marry someone they did not like.'

'I think they all knew that,' Kate said, 'but you must remember that they are still at an age when there is a lot of hormonal change going on, particularly in their bodies. So the highs of excitement are higher and their low moods lower—everything is more dramatic, exaggerated!'

Farida's mother nodded.

'You can say that again. Farida's been a drama queen for the last few years—we're just hoping we're nearly through it.'

Farida pulled a face at her mother, who answered with a loving smile, and the conversation turned more general, Kate's hostess asking about her family and how she was handling being so far away from them.

'I've worked away from home before,' Kate explained, 'and while my mother's busy at home and my brother is happy, I am content just to be in touch by phone and email. And these days it is so easy to get to anywhere in the world. Should something happen, I could be home within a couple of days.'

She felt Fareed stiffen beside her but didn't turn to look at him, still overwhelmed by seeing him in his local dress.

'Kate's mother bred and is training one of Ibrahim's horses,' Fareed told the company, and something in his voice told Kate he was wondering about her bargain.

Had he guessed?

Did it matter?

They moved in to dinner, and the conversation

turned to local and international affairs, the three young women drawing Kate into talk of shops and shopping, and making plans to take her to the mall again—

'Only this time to shop,' Suley said.

Fareed held his wife's arm as she slipped on her sandals, then continued to hold it as they went down to the car. They had said their farewells in the front vestibule, so now were alone—or as alone as they could be with a driver.

His mind played back the bits of conversation they'd had earlier. Kate's denial that Ibrahim had given her money, the talk of a bargain, then the light-bulb moment.

Or was he wrong?

Only one way to find out.

'Was your bargain with Ibrahim that your mother would train the horse?'

He was sitting close to her and felt the tension build in her body.

'Yes!'

One defiant word.

'You talk of a loving family. What did your mother think of *that*? Selling yourself so she could train a horse? How could she have allowed such a thing?'

Silence, then, 'She doesn't know.' No defiance now, more quiet resignation. 'I've worked abroad so much, when I told her I was coming here for a year she wasn't surprised.'

'And the marriage?'

More silence.

'She doesn't know about that either.'

The whispered words did something to Fareed's heart—caught at it and twisted it somehow, yet words she'd said earlier needed explanation.

He hardened the twisted heart.

'And the one year? Is that all Ibrahim asked of you? Did you intend to serve out your sentence of marriage to me then walk away?'

The questions, so coldly put, numbed Kate for a moment, but she knew she had to answer. Fareed deserved that, at least.

'I never saw it as a sentence.' She spoke quietly, trying to get through the armour Fareed had rebuilt about himself. 'I told you on our wedding night that I was happy just to work here, that as far as I was concerned we didn't need to live as man and wife, or even see each other very much, but, yes, Ibrahim had said if, after a year, we found we didn't suit, then I could leave.'

'And if I ask you to leave now?'

'I have no idea,' Kate admitted. 'I suppose I leave.'

And Ibrahim takes the horse to another trainer and breaks Billy's heart.

Her own heart ached at the thought, but at least she'd tried…

They had pulled up at the rear of the palace building and the driver once again had the door open for them.

'Unfortunately, you can't leave for forty days,' Fareed said, icicles hanging off the words.

'The forty days from our wedding?' She could understand that. To leave earlier would be to embarrass him in front of his people.

'No, forty days from today before we can divorce,' and with that he was out of the car and stalking, not into the corridor that led back to their suite but off into the night, towards the stables.

Heartsick, Kate climbed out of the car and made her own way to the suite.

Once inside she showered but the water didn't wash away the feeling of grubbiness that talking about her bargain with Ibrahim had left behind on her skin.

She pulled on her old pyjamas and climbed into bed, feeling the emptiness of it echoing the emptiness in her heart.

CHAPTER ELEVEN

HE MUST HAVE told the staff to let him know, for as soon as Kate arrived at the hospital next morning, Fareed appeared.

'I will show you around,' he said, so formally she wanted to weep.

'Did you see Ibrahim?' she asked as he led her to the back of the reception room where the radiology and pathology suites were.

'I did, and you're right, he doesn't look well, but I also spoke to his physician, who told me Ibrahim is just getting over a hepatitis attack and will be well again within weeks. He assured me that I won't need to give up my day job in the near future.'

'Oh, I'm so glad!' Kate said, feeling genuine relief that the man she liked was on the mend.

'Glad for me or him?' Fareed asked.

The question jolted Kate and this morning she really wasn't in any state to be coping with jolts.

'For him, of course. I like him.'

'And you don't like me?'

Kate stopped outside the pathology lab and shook her head as she stared at her husband.

'Now you're being downright adolescent,' she told him. 'You knew from the start this was an arrangement, now somehow my agreeing because of my family is worse than my taking money.'

He glared at her and stalked away.

'Someone else will come to show you the back section.'

Fareed knew he was behaving badly but he couldn't seem to stop.

He'd somehow come to terms with being attracted to a money-hungry female, so why was the knowledge she'd done this for her family—not for money—annoying him so much?

Because 'family' was a foreign concept to him?

Nonsense, he'd had enough family growing up—a huge family.

It might have been lacking in the loving mother and father department, but Ibrahim and his wife had never shown anything but love to him—the same love they gave their own children.

Fortunately, with Kate being shown around, the ER was busy, so he let work push all other thoughts from his head until she returned to help him with a badly dehydrated man, found lying by the side of a road in the desert.

Kate was dripping water into his mouth through a wide-bore syringe while a nurse sponged the emaciated body and he searched for a vein so he could set a catheter in place and get a saline solution flowing into him.

'Will you have to do a cut down for a wide-bore catheter?' Kate asked, thinking Fareed might have to open up the subclavian vein or internal jugular near the patient's neck to get a catheter seated and fluid flowing as swiftly as possible into the almost comatose patient.

'I'm thinking subclavian,' he responded. 'Want to do it?'

It was a challenge and she rose to it, having done a number of them in the past, usually on burn victims.

A nurse swabbed the area while Kate checked equipment and pulled on a gown and mask, then fresh gloves. Still not sure of protocol, she went with what she was used to doing and that was being sterile for even simple operations.

Fareed made no comment, busy administering a local anaesthetic around the site.

Kate moved in, feeling along the man's clavicle, finding the spot she needed along the inferior surface of it. With Fareed so close, the tension between them still twanging in the air, she worried she'd get it wrong, but the needle she'd attached to a syringe slid in beneath the skin, along the clavicle and finally into the vein.

She drew out some blood to make sure it was seated properly, then carefully detached the syringe, capping the needle she'd left in place to prevent air entering the vein.

Now for the guide wire! Carefully she inserted it into the hollow needle, advancing it into the vein then retracting it just a little. Holding the wire firmly, she withdrew the needle, then used a scalpel to stab a small hole beside the wire to enlarge the catheter site.

Now it was just a matter of threading the different pieces of equipment over the wire—first a dilator to enlarge the hole, twisting it gently as it went into the vein, then another tiny piece of plastic slid down the wire and into the dilator, taking its place so she could remove the dilator.

'You're doing well,' she heard Fareed murmur, but even the unexpected praise didn't distract her, because through every move she had to keep the wire in place while fiddling with something else. Now the catheter, down over the wire and safely into the vein. Kate checked the monitor that was showing every detail of what was going on inside the patient and sighed with relief.

Now she could withdraw the wire and cap the end of the catheter until they flushed the line, took more blood for testing then attached the IV tube and began restoring the patient's fluid balance.

Next step was to stitch the catheter into place.

'I'll take over,' Fareed told her, and she gladly handed over, realising that the tension of performing even this minor surgery with him so close had left her feeling weak-limbed and exhausted.

A nurse was labelling the blood samples and Fareed had plenty of help, so Kate headed for the bathroom, where she stripped off her gown, mask and gloves and had a good wash.

When Fareed finished, he would order an X-ray of the man's chest to make absolutely certain the catheter was in a vein and not in a nearby artery.

* * *

'All good,' he said when he caught up with her later, and as his tone sounded almost friendly, Kate began to hope his anger over her bargain might have dissipated.

But his non-appearance when she was leaving the hospital—so no lift home with him—and his absence from the suite when she did get home suggested she'd been fooling herself.

Could she really live like this?

Forty more days with a man who obviously despised her? The word came to her out of her childhood, some old book with tales of sultans and harems and women kept in isolation—purdah!

Except she didn't have to accept it.

She was reluctant to cause gossip in the palace or do anything to embarrass him with the servants, but what the hell.

She found her phone and called Mai.

'Fareed's not in this evening, so do the three of you want to come over for a swim and then some dinner?'

'In the wedding suite?' Mai asked, in almost reverent tones.

'Of course,' Kate told her.

'We'll be there as soon as we can.' Mai's excitement made Kate smile.

Kate called a servant and explained the young women were coming over, there'd be four for dinner and could it be served in the pergola in the garden at eight?

The servant didn't seem taken aback, so maybe it was okay for a woman in purdah to have friends.

Showering quickly, she put on a black bikini, thankful the garden was private as she hadn't thought to bring a full swimsuit. Over it she pulled a black-and-white patterned caftan, also brought from home because it had been a present from Billy on her last Christmas at home.

Right now she needed to feel close to her family despite her betrayal of them…

The three friends oohed and aahed over the hidden garden, then used the bathroom to change. Out in the pool they splashed like dolphins, playing in the water with such excitement Kate finally had to ask.

'Do you not have pools at home?'

Three shakes of the head.

'Our parents are very modern in some things,' Suley explained, 'but for us to be cavorting like this—no way! When we go to a pool in a hotel or even if we go to the beach, we may wear a swim-suit but we must wear our *abayas* over it, and our scarves, so we bob around in the water like big black blobs because air gets caught under our *abayas* and they blow up like balloons.'

The picture of any number of blobby women swimming in scarves and *abayas* made Kate smile.

'Well, here it's completely private so you can enjoy it all you want.'

It was the noise—the shouts of laughter and high-pitched squeals—that drew Fareed to the window.

He'd stayed back at work, telling himself it wasn't to avoid his wife but not really believing it.

Arriving home, he'd decided to find her in the suite, compliment her again on the work she'd done today then perhaps try to close the gap that had pushed them apart.

Gap?

More like a chasm.

And knowing it was his fault only made it harder. Cerebrally he knew he was at fault. The fact she'd agreed to marry him for the sake of her family should have made the so-called bargain more acceptable.

So why didn't it?

He had no idea.

Except he *had* come home hoping to make things right—or perhaps less wrong.

Which he could no longer do as she was obviously entertaining.

Pushing his feet reluctantly towards the window, he looked out into the secret garden.

His wife was sitting on one end of the pool, her tantalising body clothed in nothing but two strips of black material—making it more, not less, tantalising.

She was watching three young women frolicking in the pool, smiling at their antics and encouraging their silly behaviour. Her three young friends…

Had they come to call on her?

During her wedding month?

Unlikely—they would know the rules…

So she'd asked them over…

Not that he could blame her. She was enduring isolation she'd never have known before.

Which was his fault for not being here for her.

Al'ama—he *had* to get his head straight.

He moved away from the window, not wanting to embarrass her guests, but the sounds of laughter wormed their way inside him and he wondered how long it had been since he had laughed in such a carefree way.

He called a servant, and learned that the friends were staying for dinner.

Caution suggested he go for a ride and eat later in his dressing room, but instead he asked the servant to take a message to his wife, advising her he was home for dinner and suggesting he join her and her friends in the pergola.

Would she refuse?

He doubted it. She was still so uncertain about their customs she would probably take the suggestion as an order.

Was it wrong for him to take advantage of her this way?

For sure, but what the hell. Why *shouldn't* he eat with his wife and her friends? Laugh with his wife and her friends?

Silently acknowledging that he'd somehow got himself into an impossible situation, he headed for his bathroom, showered, then put on traditional clothes—'at home' traditional in the form of a simple white robe.

Because she admired you in traditional garb yesterday? an imp whispered in his head.

He refused to answer it, merely waiting in his study off his private bedroom until the dinner was carried out into the pergola.

The friends greeted him with kisses and apparent glee, his wife more calmly, although he thought he detected a gleam of surprise in her eyes when she saw how he was dressed.

She poured him juice then looked at the pretty women lounging under the pergola, dressed now in jeans and tops—the uniform of youth.

'Now tell me this,' she said, addressing her visitors but waving one hand towards him as she spoke. 'You have to cover up—wear *abayas* and scarves—when you go to the mall, and even when you swim at the beach, but here, now Fareed has joined us, you don't have to cover up?'

They laughed and all tried to explain at once.

Fareed held up his hand.

'They are family. They can appear uncovered in front of the men in their family, their fathers, brothers and in my case even cousins because I grew up with them—well, not exactly but I've known them all their lives.'

He knew by the little frown between her eyebrows that Kate wasn't satisfied.

'But when marriages are arranged, aren't they often within the family—to cousins or second cousins? I'm sure Suley's mother mentioned that,' she said.

'It's different with cousins our own age,' Farida explained. 'We might have played with them when we were little but now, if they're around, we cover up. Fareed's more like an uncle so he doesn't matter.'

'Well, thank you very much!' Fareed said, but he was pleased to see Kate smiling at the remark.

Maybe things weren't broken beyond repair.

Why had he joined them?

Kate ate and talked—well, listened—all the time so aware of Fareed she could feel her skin tingling. Fooling around with the friends, teasing them, asking questions about their studies, offering advice in a casual way, she saw a side of him she hadn't seen before.

Fareed, the family man?

Not really, just Fareed the man.

Up until now he'd been a stranger, then her husband but still a stranger, then a colleague and a lover...

She shivered at the memories of the lover, and her body grew warm beneath her all-encompassing caftan.

But Fareed the lover was gone and in thirty-nine days Fareed the husband would also be gone.

Thirty-nine days alone in that big bed...

Couldn't they at least enjoy the unexpected attraction that had flared between them like a forest fire?

Look on it as a holiday romance?

Oh, yeah, and just how are you going to put it to him?

I know you hate me for making the arrangement with Ibrahim but could we at least sleep together until I go?

Like that would happen!

Coldness now where the warmth had been, and Fareed bringing her out of her thoughts—back to the present.

'Our guests are leaving,' he said—oh, so smooth, so suave when they'd been *her* guests, not *theirs*.

She walked behind the other four towards their suite then accompanied her visitors to the front door, where their driver was waiting.

Fareed stopped at the door, kissed and hugged the threesome, then disappeared back into the palace while Kate saw them into the car.

'So much for suggesting we enjoy a holiday romance,' she muttered to herself as she made her way back to the suite.

Angry and unhappy, she slipped back out into the garden, heading for the pergola where she could sit and think.

Except it was already occupied.

'You enjoy their company?'

The voice of her husband—an unnecessary question, surely, so what was he really asking?

'They are fun,' Kate replied, moving past the pergola to stand by the side of the pool.

'And I'm not?'

The anger Kate really didn't understand fired up again.

'How would I know?' she demanded. 'I barely know you, any more than you know me! Oh, you're quite happy to judge me, but actually getting to know me—perhaps that isn't part of marriage over here.'

'Getting to know someone takes time.'

He sounded so calm she wanted to throw something at him.

'Time together, not time apart,' she said. 'Anyway, it doesn't matter—there's no point in us getting to know each other now. Only thirty-nine more days and I'll be out of your hair and you can get on with enjoying whatever life you were leading before I came into it.'

Silence that stretched and stretched, eventually for so long Kate took a step back towards the pergola, peering into the shadows so she could make out his form, check he was still there.

She was one step closer when he finally spoke.

'There wasn't much enjoyment in it, my old life,' he said quietly, and Kate took the steps she needed to join him in the shadows, sitting down beside him, taking his hand, holding it in both of hers.

'Tell me,' she said, and as he had the evening at the fort, slowly and carefully he did.

Telling her the things he'd thought were fun— buying the fastest of cars and racing them along empty desert roads, vying with his cousins for affairs with glamorous women, university studies overseas where he'd tried alcohol and drugs, partying wildly…

'In the hope of having fun,' he finished quietly.

'But at the time it must have been good,' Kate protested, and heard a smile in his voice as he answered.

'Oh, yes, at the time I thought it very good, but it was empty fun, Kate—bought fun. If you have money you can buy anything.'

'Even a wife,' she whispered, and he stood up and walked away, pacing at the end of the pool.

'That's different,' he said harshly. 'It's our custom—there is always a bride gift—brides *are* bought.'

She'd felt so close to him but now?

She could let it go and maybe he'd sit again, they could recover what they'd lost…

But she had to know.

'So why was my arrangement with Ibrahim so upsetting for you?'

'Because it was family business and Ibrahim knew how I felt about family, and to put us in that suite, redecorated or not… I found my father's body in that suite—his body and a note that destroyed any illusion I might have had about my loving family!'

She moved swiftly to his side, putting her hand on his arm.

'Why? How? What did the note say that made you feel that way?'

He spun towards her, his eyes glittering in the moonlight.

'You really want to know?'

She nodded, and though he turned away from her again she heard the words ring clearly through the night air.

'It wasn't addressed to anyone,' he began, 'but I was the first to read it. It said, "She doesn't love me, never did, and cares for Fareed even less. My death will end both my pain and my beloved son's so it is best I do this."'

Kate shook her head as she tried to process the words. She wanted nothing more than to hold him but he was already striding away, away from her and their marriage and towards the place that held such horrific memories for him.

'Well, you *had* to know!' she muttered to herself, then she returned to the pergola, sank down on the cushions and considered whether a good cry would help.

Not in the slightest—all it would do was make her eyes all red and puffy!

So she thought instead, thought about Fareed and the ghosts Ibrahim had told her of, wondered just where he'd found his father.

Surely not in the big marriage bed.

His mother must have used it—the big bed. She had seen it as her right so his father had probably used the bedroom off Fareed's dressing room—rooms she'd never seen.

Of course, he might not have gone to bed, but if he had, could she let him sleep alone in there with the memories she'd evoked so unthinkingly fresh in his mind?

He'd been a child.

A lost child, for all the family love around him.

She sighed, got off the cushions, left the garden, took a shower, pulled on a robe, then went in search of her husband.

The room she found was dark, but once her eyes adjusted to the gloom she could make out the form of a body—a live body, she was sure—beneath the covers.

Coming closer, she slipped off the robe and slid between the sheets, reaching out a tentative hand, finding an arm and resting her hand on it, stroking lightly.

A movement told her he wasn't asleep so she slid closer, put her arms around his body, pressing herself against his back.

'We don't have to make love, Fareed, but I guessed this was the bed, and I didn't want you sleeping in it alone when I've hurt you by bringing back those memories.'

She said no more, just lay there, spooned against an unyielding body.

At least he hadn't kicked her out, and this felt so good, just being close to him.

CHAPTER TWELVE

HE WAS GONE when she woke in the morning, disoriented and confused. At some time during the night he'd turned to her, touched her, arousing her desire so she'd responded fully and completely, so a frantic coupling had been followed by a slow, seductive, teasing act of what to Kate had been love.

Freed from all inhibitions by the knowledge that soon she'd lose this man, she'd let her hands explore him fully, let her lips brush against his smooth skin, let her teeth nibble at his ear, his shoulder and let her tongue wander at will, finally arousing him again, so that time, in her mind, they'd made love.

But this morning he was gone, and soon she'd be going, and in the meantime she should get to work.

Or not?

The thought occurred to her as she stood under the shower, rinsing conditioner from her hair.

At least at work she'd see him, if only across

the room, and hear his voice, if only from another cubicle. To not see him, to not hear him, to not take whatever she could of him for these last few weeks would be unbearable.

Don't be pathetic, woman!

Get a grip!

You'll go to work because at the moment it's still your job and other people are relying on you.

And you will not get all weak-kneed over seeing him or hearing his bloody voice.

Kate sighed and did pull herself together, though reluctantly. She plaited her still-wet hair, slapped moisturiser on her face, dressed in her usual work uniform of jeans and a shirt, and sat down at the table where her breakfast had been set.

Without being ordered?

She checked it out—fruit, yoghurt, cereal, cof-fee—exactly what she usually ordered, so perhaps the servants simply brought it now.

Except there was a red rosebud in a tiny silver vase, right in the middle of the tray.

Fareed?

She shook her head and told her heart to not get overexcited, but somewhere inside, a tiny bud of hope, much smaller than the rosebud, began to unfurl a tentative leaf.

Which withered and died when she arrived at work to find her husband wasn't on duty.

'The boss does his prince-of-the-realm thing on the first Tuesday of the month,' Roberta told her. 'Didn't he tell you? He sits with the sultan and people come and tell them their troubles and they sort it out. It's a tradition, going back for ever.'

Of course he hadn't told her, not that or anything about his 'prince' life.

It was realising just how little she knew of him that killed the bud.

Fareed tried to listen to the supplicants as they told their stories to Ibrahim, but his mind kept wandering—to the previous night, to the need to talk to Ibrahim, to working out exactly where his marriage was…

Or wasn't!

He'd offered her a divorce—actually, demanded more than offered—told her that in forty days—thirty-eight now—she could go back to the family that meant so much to her.

It would be for the best. He'd marry again, someone from his own culture. Ibrahim of all people should have known how disastrous mixed marriages could be.

Yet Ibrahim had planned this...

He must have sighed, for the supplicant in front of them turned to him, assuring him it wasn't such a big problem and that all would be well.

'Would that it could be,' Fareed told him, then realised he'd spoken in English and changed his translation to a blessing for the man.

He came in late in the afternoon, striding into the ER with an injured child in his arms, issuing orders as he carried the child into a cubicle, sending nurses scurrying to help.

Kate followed him into the cubicle, where he was placing the little boy carefully down on the examination couch, his hands gentle as he spread the small limbs.

'What happened?' Kate asked.

He didn't glance her way, intent on examining the boy.

'One of those idiots on a motorbike—the young men with too much money and not enough to do with their time who sit outside the malls on women's shopping days, revving their bikes to make the teenage girls notice them. He was swerving through the crowd near the market and hit the child a glancing blow, sending him flying into a market stall. Didn't even stop!'

Kate heard the anger in his voice and understood it. How could anyone be, first, so careless and then so uncaring?

'Did no one come forward to claim him?'

Fareed shook his head.

'There are people searching for his parents, asking through the markets, but I think he may have been a beggar, possibly the child of a migrant worker who either didn't want him or who died. It happens, although there are services out there that usually pick up children like this and take them into care, find caring foster-families for them.'

He finished his examination, found a vein in the child's arm and took some blood, all the time talking quietly to the boy, although he was unconscious.

'Let's take him through to Radiology, see what an X-ray tells us.'

Not having anything else to do, Kate followed, realising how much she enjoyed watching Fareed in action as a doctor.

A caring doctor!

Just one more thing about him she'd have to forget.

The X-rays revealed a hairline crack in the base of his skull, which explained his concussion.

Further tests showed no bleeding or swelling in his brain, yet he remained comatose.

'I'll keep him here and stay with him. I'm sure he was conscious when I picked him up—I was right behind the motorbike when it happened—so at least I might be a familiar face to him.'

Kate started to remind him that with concussion most patients remembered little of what had happened during and straight after an accident—or even just prior to it—but she stopped herself, realising Fareed would stay there whatever she said.

So no night of love, not that night or the next. No rosebuds on her breakfast tray, and no communication outside of work.

She caught him in the staff room three days later, where he was cursing the coffee machine.

'How's the little boy?' she asked, as she took over from him, bumping the machine on the left side, a trick she'd learned that would make it work.

'How did you do that?' he demanded, and she

showed him, trying desperately to remain as cool and in control as he was, although her body wanted nothing more than to melt against him.

She handed him a coffee, got one for herself, and took it to a lounge chair, needing a break after a busy morning.

'The little boy?' she asked, when she realised Fareed was still hovering in the room.

'I've had him admitted to the hospital. He's still unconscious, although scans of his brain tell us there's nothing wrong there, and his blood tests have come back normal.'

'How old would you say he is?'

'The paediatrician says five or six, although he's small for his age.'

Kate thought about a child that age left to roam the streets.

'Do you think subconsciously he doesn't want to come out of his coma? Do you think he could just have closed down? If you think how bad his life must have been, maybe this is a nice way of avoiding it.'

Fareed stared at her.

'Do you think humans have the power to do that?'

Kate shrugged.

'I don't know but we all try to block out bad things that happen in our lives, yet we still remember them, probably more than the good memories. And who knows what he might need to block out?'

Fareed didn't answer, simply finishing his coffee and leaving the room.

Two more nights in purdah, although by now Kate had convinced herself she didn't care.

So why, when he did appear in the suite after dinner on the third night, grave-faced and stern, did her heart leap in her chest and her blood rush hotly through her veins.

He hasn't come for fun, she told her errant body, and she crossed to the window, looking out at the garden that had become her refuge, knowing, somehow, that this might be her last view of it.

'Ibrahim has heard from his man in Australia,' Fareed said, then must have seen her shock for he immediately added, 'No, your family is all right, it is the horse. Apparently some hooligans were out with guns—rifles, probably—shooting in the bush. They shot the horse.'

'Shot Tippy?'

Kate sank down into a chair and stared blindly at the bearer of bad news.

Fareed nodded.

'What about Billy? Is Billy all right?' She stood up again, panicky now. 'He would have been with Tippy, surely?'

'As far as I know, your brother wasn't injured.'

Kate nodded while her brain kept throwing up any number of consequences Tippy's death might have had on Billy.

'I'll phone home,' she said to Fareed. 'I might have to go, to help Mum with Billy, with the stables probably. Ibrahim won't leave his men there now.'

'And, of course, your "bargain" with him is null and void?'

Kate stared at her husband, unable to believe he'd spoken so coldly. They might not be friends but they had shared some passion.

'I wasn't thinking of that, but of helping my family,' she said, her own voice as cold as she could make it. 'Something you wouldn't understand because although you had all the love Ibrahim and *his* family could give you, you kept yourself apart, nursing the hurt your own parents did to you, peeling the scabs off the scars so you could continue to feel sorry for yourself. Don't you realise you've got to put it all behind you? Yes, you were hurt, but pain is part of being alive, you get over it and move on—how else can you become the best you possibly can be when you're letting the past cripple you?'

'You don't know me,' he said, his anger so tight it seemed to suck the air out of the room.

'I know enough to know you're a fine man, a caring man, and a wonderful doctor, but you could be so much more if you would just let go of all the anger seething inside you.'

She moved closer, stood in front of him, looked into the dark, dark eyes.

'You talk about freedom, Fareed. Free yourself from the past, from the ghosts that take up far too much space in your head.'

For a moment she thought she might have got through to him but, no, he turned his back on her and stalked out of the room, pausing at the door.

'You know nothing of me. Go home to your family!'

His words pierced her heart, leaving her shaken by his coldness. Not that she hadn't asked for it, bringing up all the things he'd told her in confidence, telling him he had to get a life!

But even so, before she'd spoken, could he not have offered just a little comfort? Asked her if she needed help to make arrangements? Suggested she return?

Well, that last was never going to happen. He was probably glad of a reason to get rid of her before the forty days were up.

A knock at the door—a servant summoning her to Ibrahim.

Kate followed the young woman through the endless passages of the palace, coming at last to a small study where Ibrahim sat in a leather lounge chair. He rose as she entered, taking her hand to lead her to a chair beside his.

'I have spoken to your mother. She had trouble getting hold of you at the hospital so she phoned the palace. You will want to talk to her yourself and can phone her when you get back to your suite. But I can tell you your brother is all right—unhappy, but your mother thinks he will handle it, although when I suggested you would probably want to be with them, she was very relieved.'

'Thank you, Ibrahim. I do need to be with them.'

'My plane is being prepared as we speak,' he said, 'and will take off in three hours. Your driver will take you to the airport, unless your husband wishes to drive you.'

Kate looked into the kindly eyes of the older man. 'I somehow doubt that,' she said.

'He is a fool!' Ibrahim muttered. 'A fool not to see how happy the two of you could be together. He has told me he intends divorce, but it cannot happen for forty days, my dear, so if you wish to return...'

'To a man who doesn't care for me?' Kate tried to smile but her lips wobbled and she breathed deeply instead, not wanting to cry in front of Ibrahim.

'You must do what you think best,' Ibrahim told her, patting her hand.

So once again she was up in the air, in the luxurious jet, heading home at a million miles an hour, heartsore at leaving, angry at herself for being stupid enough to fall in love.

Because that was what she'd done. She'd fallen in love with a man who'd been tricked into marrying her and to whom she was everything he most disliked in a woman—foreign, red-haired, out for what she could get...

She tried to think of Billy, of how he must be feeling, coping. Told herself her pain was nothing but self-pity, and she had to think of others, not herself.

But the 'other' who crept into her head wasn't her

mother, or Billy, but Fareed. Fareed on his beautiful stallion, king of the desert over which he rode. Fareed at work, so calm and competent, caring enough for the little boy to stay with him overnight…

Fareed who didn't love her, and why should he? They barely knew each other…

She slept and woke in airspace over Australia—home.

He got through one day, but the night was too much. They may not have slept together the previous few nights as he'd been at the hospital but he still felt her presence in the suite.

He was tortured by her presence in the suite!

Yet he'd let her go without a mention of that torture, without telling her he'd miss her or asking her if she'd come back—without offering to go with her, to support her as a husband should.

At midnight he phoned the airport, arranged for a plane to be made ready, a pilot organised, a flight plan registered. He'd leave at dawn.

Kate arrived home in one of the big black limousines that had brought Ibrahim and Fareed to the stud the first time, people from the embassy having met her at the airport.

'You didn't have to come,' her mother said, although the hug she gave Kate told her otherwise.

'Billy?' Kate asked, and her mother shook her head.

'I don't know what to do with him,' she admitted. 'He sits on the deck and looks out at Tippy's paddock, not speaking, barely eating. The mares are due to start foaling so I'm busy with them as well as the horses in work and can't give him the attention he probably needs, but I don't know how to help him.'

Kate gave her mother another hug and went to find her brother. She'd been seven when Billy had been born, a baby she'd looked forward to with all her heart. A real, live doll had been how she'd thought of him. Except he'd come too early, and the doll had been a wizened little thing in an incubator. So many premmie babies did well, they'd all hoped for the best, and when he hadn't reached his milestones, not talking or attempting to walk, her parents had put it down to her doing everything for him, interpreting his wishes before he'd had a chance to talk, carrying him around with her.

But it had been more than that. Investigations had shown a rare syndrome, a debilitating condition that meant he was slow to develop, and vulnerable to illness. It hadn't been until he'd been six that he'd discovered an affinity with the horses, spending all his time following his parents around the stables and yards, starting to speak so he could talk to his 'friends'.

Then Tippy! Tippy had been special...

'It hurts, doesn't it Billy, to lose something you love?'

She pulled a chair over close to him, refused to think of being here with Ibrahim, and took her brother's hand.

'First Dad, and now Tippy. I know you're sad but Mum probably needs you in the stables. The mares are due to start foaling—you usually help her.'

Billy shook his head.

'Isaac will help her.'

It took Kate a minute to realise Isaac was the man Ibrahim had organised to work at the stables—and had been paying for!

'Is he still here?' Kate asked, and Billy nodded.

'Him and Tony. Tony is my friend.'

Perhaps Ibrahim was going to ease them out of

their employment here, Kate thought, but aloud she said, 'Then couldn't you be helping him?'

'Don't want to!'

Billy in a stubborn mood, Kate knew it well.

'Okay,' she said, 'although I wouldn't mind going down to have a look around. Come with me?'

The shake of his head told Kate it was the end of the conversation, but she *did* need to go down to the stables, to talk to her mother and find out why Ibrahim's men were still here.

That conversation didn't happen, as Isaac and the young lad called Tony were both down at the mares' paddock with her mother, and she could hardly talk about it in front of them.

'We're checking on them because there's a big race meeting in Sydney this weekend and we've got Tippy's brother and two other horses entered in races,' Sally explained. 'I feel bad leaving you when you've just arrived but I'm so glad you're here because I really want to see these three race and I couldn't have left Billy otherwise.'

'Of course you should go, Mum,' Kate said. 'It will be good for me to have some together time with Billy anyway.'

Her mother still looked worried.

'Mum! It's not as if the mares don't usually manage on their own and I know the vet's number off by heart if anything untoward happens. Just go and enjoy yourself. Once the foals arrive and the mares are being mated again, you won't have a spare moment.'

Kate hoped she sounded firm enough, although being left with—she counted quickly—eleven pregnant mares was slightly daunting.

Her mother turned and hugged her.

'Thank you,' she said, then she slipped through the fence and walked around the animals, talking softly to them, probably, Kate realised, telling them who'd be in charge over the weekend. Billy wasn't the only one who talked to the horses!

The horses going to the races left early the next morning, so when Kate toured the stables at what she considered the early hour of seven o'clock, they were quiet.

Old Josh, who'd been with them for as long as she could remember, greeted her with a horsy-smelling hug.

'Your mum's doing real well,' he told her. 'We've got owners from all over asking her to take their horses for training. I'm taking this fellow to the locals tomorrow, and the mare in the stall next to him will go to the midweeks in town.'

He walked her through the old building, introducing her to the new horses, but Kate was more interested in trying to work out what was different about the place, other than the new horses.

It still smelled of horse, and liniment and tack polish, but…

Was it tidier in some way?

Her mother had always tried to keep things tidy, insisting on everything being in its rightful place, but somehow there'd always been a saddle stuck on a rail somewhere, and a bridle hanging from a nail on the wall of a stall.

And clean—the place was almost spotless—another condition her mother had aimed at but rarely achieved.

'Everything looks good,' Kate said to Josh, who smiled and nodded.

'That Isaac, he's a quiet man, but he sees the jobs get done. Just what you mother needed, someone with a firm hand.'

And for the first time Kate wondered just how her mother had managed, taking care of the horses, the business paperwork and the family, while Dad, wonderful as he'd been, had been off chasing his dreams.

Thinking about this, she wandered down to the mares' paddock, slipped through the fence, then walked around them, talking quietly, checking for signs of imminent delivery—wax on their teats or milk leaking from them, restlessness, walking round in circles, shaking their legs, lying down and standing up again.

These were the signs her mother had told her to watch for, although now she stood in the paddock with the mares it all came back to her from the times she'd done the same thing with her mother.

'Not that they all show any of the signs,' Kate remembered her mother saying as she climbed back through the fence. She'd check them again this evening and in the meantime she'd have another talk to Billy.

Billy still wasn't talking so Kate occupied herself making a huge pot of chicken soup that could be frozen in portions ready to be heated when needed. With mares usually foaling in the early hours of the morning, the humans checking them would often need hot food at odd hours of the night.

Once that was on she made her way down to a smaller shed behind the stables where two birthing stalls had been set up. The large stalls were spotless and had bales of hay ready to be spread. Although her mother preferred to leave the mares in the paddock to foal, if there was an emergency and they needed the vet, it was easier to bring them here where there was good light.

Satisfied everything was in order but desperate for work to keep her mind off the life—and husband—she'd left behind, she found the paint she'd been using on the fences and took it out to continue the never-ending job.

Within an hour Billy had joined her, arriving with his own paintbrush, working with her on the other side of the fence, still silent but at least he was there.

Fareed sat on the plane, his mind running over the tumultuous month since he'd first met Katya.

The woman on the horse, later calling him a big lunk because he'd been struggling against her, her lips on his, breathing life into his lungs.

Then the parcel that was his bride.

His fury at Ibrahim for doing this to him.

Except it hadn't all been fury. Right from the

moment he'd seen her there'd been something—a connection—

No, he had to be imagining that!

Although he'd certainly been attracted to the termagant he'd unwrapped, his body stirring at the sight of the pale skin, golden underwear barely covering anything…

He shook his head as he remembered his anger at the deception—anger at her and at Ibrahim. Kate—sensible Kate—had been right about him holding on to his unhappy childhood memories, using them as a shield against love.

Was it too late to woo and win her now?

He knew he wanted to—more than wanted, needed to.

The realisation that Ibrahim—and the old crone, Thalia—had been right in choosing her for him still didn't sit comfortably with him, yet in his heart of hearts he knew they were right.

Katya definitely was the woman for him; now all he had to do was convince her of that.

Billy and Kate had chicken soup for dinner, phoned their mother to check she'd arrived safely at the city stables and the horses had settled in, then went out, torches in hand, to check the mares again.

Kate knew her mother walked among the mares several times a day, so they were used to someone being there. Tonight she pulled on her mother's coat, knowing she wouldn't fool the mares but hoping the scent of it would be reassuring to them.

'The problem is,' she said to Billy as they walked down the track, 'that a mare can stop her labour if she's disturbed—sometimes stop it for several days—and that's not good for her or the foal.'

To her surprise, Billy actually responded.

'I know that,' he said, and Kate could have hugged him, although she refrained, guessing he, too, needed his own space right now.

They walked among the mares, talking quietly.

'Sarina's restless,' Billy said, pointing to Tippy's mother, moving a little apart from the others.

'We won't go near her,' Kate said, 'but I'll come down again later to check on her.'

'Me, too. Don't go without me,' Billy said, and this time Kate *did* put an arm around his narrow shoulders and give him a hug.

Back home she suggested they go to bed. She

set the alarm to wake in three hours and prayed she'd made the right decision.

Fareed had arrived in Sydney midafternoon but getting out of the city then finding his way to the stud, even with the latest GPS, took him until close to midnight.

Fortunately he could see lights on in the house as he drove down the long, fenced track towards it because only now had it occurred to him that people might not appreciate a visitor arriving in the middle of the night.

But the house was empty—unlocked and obviously with people in residence, for a smell of toast still lingered in the kitchen and butter, jam, and dirty toast plates were on the table.

Two plates?

Kate and her mother having a midnight chat?

About the marriage perhaps?

Confession time?

Shaking the thoughts from his head, he walked out onto the deck and saw the property spread before him in the moonlight. And down towards the stream two flickering lights.

Torches?

What he should do was drive back to the town where he'd been hospitalised and spend the rest of the night in a motel, but torches in a paddock this late at night suggested there might be trouble.

Forgetting what he should do, he headed towards the lights, following a track down towards the river.

Hadn't it been down here somewhere he'd met the bee—or the bee had met him? They'd been going to the mares' paddock. He tried to think whether he knew how pregnant the mares had been, but couldn't remember a thing except Katya's face bent over him, telling him to calm down, holding him, breathing into his mouth, her lips on his for the first time…

He lengthened his stride, chasing away the silly fantasies, and as he drew closer called out a quiet hello.

'Is that you, Josh?' Kate answered—definitely sensible Kate, not his seductive Katya.

'It's Fareed,' he said, close enough now to see two shadowy forms walking a horse round and round in a corner of the paddock.

He heard Kate's sharp intake of breath then she used it to breathe his name.

'Fareed?'

He'd reached the fence and now he stood, leaning over the top rail, aware that if the mare was foaling, another intruder might startle her.

'Keep walking her, Billy,' she said quietly, before coming towards him in the darkness, lowering her torch so she could pick her way to the fence.

'Why are you here?' she asked, but seeing her face in the moonlight, her eyes wide behind her glasses, his chest grew tight and his throat thickened and all the things he'd rehearsed saying on the plane flew off into the night air.

He reached out and touched her cheek, ran his hand over her hair and finally found his voice.

'I forgot to ask you if you'd come back—if you'd please come back?'

Even in the moonlight he could see her frown, and his nerves tightened.

It was too late!

He'd lost her!

Then, her eyes on his, she murmured, 'Back to Amberach or back to you?'

He had to say it—needed to say it, needed her to hear it. Drew in a deep breath, 'Back to—'

'Kate! Come now.'

She slipped away, walking swiftly towards the mare and her attendant.

'It's okay, Billy, let her lie down. That was her waters breaking, so the foal will come soon.'

The mare lay on the grass in the corner of the paddock, but even from the fence Fareed saw the red bubble protruding from her vulva. The placenta was being delivered first and without it the foal would have no oxygen.

He clambered through the fence, saying urgently, 'Bill, go up to the stables as quickly as you can and bring back the first-aid box. You know where it is?'

'Of course,' the young man answered, vaulting the fence and sprinting towards the stables.

"What's happening?' Kate asked, looking up anxiously from where she knelt beside the mare.

Fareed explained, slipping one arm around her as he spoke, giving her a quick hug.

'I've seen it before, helped the mare deliver, back at home,' he assured her, as Billy returned with the first-aid kit.

'Watch this, Bill, in case you ever have to do it yourself. We just cut through this sac—a lot of blood will come out—but after we make the opening, the mare will be able to deliver normally. You just have to do it really quickly but be careful you don't go deep enough to cut the foal's leading leg.'

By the time he'd finished explaining to Billy, he'd pulled on gloves, unwrapped a scalpel and was preparing to cut. Setting aside his awareness of Katya right behind him, he sliced the placenta and eased it to one side, then breathed a sigh of relief as he felt the little hoof already coming through the birth canal. The second foreleg was right where it should be, tucked neatly behind it.

'Here's the head,' Billy said, and within five minutes the foal was on the ground, waving spindly legs as it tried to right itself, finally getting up and staggering around in a circle before finding its mother—his mother—and nuzzling at her teat.

Sarina was on her feet, turning to lick at her baby.

'I'd let them be,' Fareed said, as he wrapped the soiled scalpel in several layers of elastic tape to protect from accidental injury then putting it and his soiled gloves into a plastic bag.

'Do you have some place to dispose of sharps?' he said to Billy, but Kate answered for her brother.

'I'll do it,' she said, and Fareed knew she was escaping—from him or from what his arrival might mean to her.

In the time he'd known her he'd given her no indication of how he felt about her, now here he was asking her to return to him.

Not that he'd known how he felt about her until she'd gone…

Billy was talking to him, asking questions about horses, how he, Fareed, knew things like that, what horses did he have, and, finally, would he take Kate away again?

'Would you mind?' Fareed asked him.

'I would miss her,' Billy said, 'but I'm really good on social networks now so we can talk and send each other pictures so she's not really gone and maybe one day I could visit her over there.'

'I'm sure she'd like that,' Fareed told him. 'But you'll probably have to wait until this little foal is older. He's going to need you to show him all the things you showed Tippy.'

'Tippy died.'

The sadness in his voice caught Fareed unawares, but he knew he had to say something.

'People and animals do die, Bill,' he said gently, 'and it's right to be sad about that. But there are always more things coming along, like this new foal, so we have to keep going to give the very best we can to the people and animals that are here.'

He hadn't done the very best he could for Katya—had been so resentful, he hadn't been able to think straight. And here she was.

'The vet's on his way. I phoned him in case there was some placenta retained inside Sarina. He said you did exactly the right thing but the placenta coming away like that is usually a sign of an infection. He wants to check her and the foal out.'

She sat down on the grass a little away from the two men, her knees up and her arms looped around her legs.

'Kate's sad,' Billy said, and Fareed turned to look at his wife. 'She's been sad since she came home.'

Kate wished she could strangle her brother, but as he seemed to be speaking freely for the first time since she'd got back, she couldn't stop him now.

She could say she was sad over Tippy, but couldn't bring herself to tell a lie—or even a half lie—because she *was* upset that the horse had been killed.

Instead, she rested her head on her knees and hoped they'd think she was having a sleep while they waited for the vet.

But Billy had other ideas.

'When I'm sad, Mum gives me a hug. You could give her a hug, couldn't you, Fareed?'

Murder wouldn't be enough, Kate thought, but she sensed movement then a body lowered to sit beside her and a strong arm came around her shoulders.

'Were you sad?' Fareed whispered to her, and she lifted her head enough to nod.

'Because of leaving Amberach or leaving me?' he asked, and now she lifted her head right up and looked at his face, so clear and dear in the moonlight.

'I think I asked that question first,' she said, and although he looked puzzled for a moment, she saw his face clear and something spark in his eyes.

'Back to me is my answer,' he said, the words so definite, she had to believe him.

'Now your turn,' he prompted.

'Both,' Kate said, smiling because she knew it wasn't the answer he wanted to hear. She touched his face, which had grown stern again. 'Even in such a short time I'd grown to love both the place and the people.' She sighed then turned so she could kiss him gently on the lips. 'And to love you, awkward sod that you are.'

* * *

With Sarina and her foal safely medicated, they finally made their way back to the house as dawn was breaking.

'You'll have to sleep in the spare room,' Kate told Fareed as they reached the house. 'Billy seems to be okay but I wouldn't want to shock him by us sleeping together.'

Fareed held her tightly and groaned.

'I imagine I can wait one more night to get you alone,' he whispered against her neck, his warm breath sending spirals of delight right through her body.

Waking at midday, Kate went down to check on the new arrival, finding Josh, Fareed and Billy there before her. Billy was already in love with the foal he'd helped deliver.

'If everything's okay I'm going up to the house to make lunch, then we can watch the races on television. You guys coming?'

'I'll stay here and watch with Josh on the stable's TV. There'll be some food in the fridge there,' Billy said, then to Kate's utter amazement he added, 'And call me Bill now, please, Kate. I am a grown-up, you know, and Billy is a name for a kid.'

'Probably my fault,' Fareed said, slipping an arm around Kate's waist as they walked up to the house. 'I called him Bill last night and he's right, really, he's ready to be a Bill.'

Kate turned and kissed him.

'You are a wise man,' she said.

He kissed her back, not a thankyou kiss like she'd bestowed on him but a loving, tender, exploration of her mouth, her lips, her tongue, his strong arms holding her hard against his body, while his lips told her everything she'd ever wanted to know. 'Not wise enough,' he told her when he'd finally released her, 'to realise just what a gift Ibrahim had given me in my wife. You were right, I was so tied up in the past I couldn't see the present. And although I was attracted to you from the beginning, I wouldn't let myself fall in love with you—'

'Because you saw your mother in me. I understood that, Fareed, yet somehow Ibrahim knew that we were meant to be. The man's a genius.'

Fareed pushed some strands of the brilliant red hair off Katya's face.

'He did have help,' he said, smiling at her. 'You might not believe this—in fact, I didn't when he told me just before I came out here this time—but he'd been worried about me, about the things that had happened in the past and how they had affected my life, so he'd called in a *kahin*—a fortune-teller—to ask what to do, and she threw sticks on the sand or poured oil on a dish of water and somehow came up with the idea that if he took me on a journey with him to a foreign country he would find a wife for me and never have to worry about me again.'

'A fortune-teller told him that?'

Kate looked at him in complete disbelief.

'But how did he know I was the one? You must have met other women while you were in Australia.'

'Dozens,' Fareed told her with a smile, 'but Thalia—the old *kahin*—kept talking about things green and Ibrahim says as soon as he saw you on the horse in the green paddocks he knew you were the one. After that it was just a matter of getting you to agree.'

'Which, once he saw how rundown the place was, wasn't really a challenge.'

Fareed drew her close, and felt her body fit to his as if they'd been designed to be together. He looked around at the green of the place, and decided green wasn't nearly as bad as he'd thought it.

'Food,' Kate said, pushing away from him. 'If we don't go now we'll miss the first race.'

In the kitchen, with a television perched on top of the refrigerator, Kate made sandwiches while he watched the beginning of the TV coverage of the afternoon's races. He'd rather be taking her to bed after their lunch but the races were important to her and her family and, now he was part of that family, important to him.

So they sat and ate the simple meal, cheered the first of the stable's horses to a win, groaned as the second one lost, then moved into the living room where there was a mammoth TV, to watch the big race of the day.

To Fareed's surprise, he was on his feet, jumping up and down as much as Katya, as the horse swept to the outside and flew to the finish line a head in front of the second horse.

Flushed and excited, his wife flung herself into his arms, hugging and kissing him, stopping only when the phone rang, her mother phoning home.

'Sarina foaled last night, a little colt, and Fareed's here,' Kate said, unable to keep this most exciting arrival a secret from her mother.

'Ah,' her mother said. 'I gathered from constant mentions in your emails that he might be something more than your boss. But just how long were you going to wait before you told me more about him?'

'Mu-u-u-m,' Kate said. 'I've barely seen you.'

'We'll talk about it later, but I'm so glad for you, darling,' her mother said.

'I will have a lot of explaining to do,' she muttered to herself, looking so worried Fareed took her in his arms again.

'We'll do it together,' he promised. 'How about a whirlwind romance then, because of my position, we married? We can offer to do it again here.'

He looked into her eyes.

'In fact, I'd like to do it again, do it properly, your way, holding your hand and promising to love, honour and obey you for ever.'

Kate kissed his lips.

'I think we'll both leave out the obey bit,' she teased, then as tears of happiness threatened to spill from her eyes she nestled close to him, aware that this was where she wanted to be.

Forever…

* * * * *

R